Old Quarrels, Old Love

Storybook written by

Heather Conkie

Based on the Sullivan Films Production
adapted from the novels of

Lucy Maud Montgomery

A BANTAM SKYLARK BOOK®
NEW YORK • TORONTO • LONDON • SYDNEY • AUCKLAND

*Based on the Sullivan Films Production produced by Sullivan Films Inc.
in association with CBC and the Disney Channel with the participation
of Telefilm Canada adapted from Lucy Maud Montgomery's novels.*

*Teleplay written by Heather Conkie.
Copyright © 1991 by Sullivan Films Distribution, Inc.*

*This edition contains the complete text
of the original edition.*
NOT ONE WORD HAS BEEN OMITTED.

RL 6, 008–012

OLD QUARRELS, OLD LOVE
*A Bantam Skylark Book / published by arrangement with
HarperCollins Publishers Ltd.*

PUBLISHING HISTORY
*HarperCollins edition published 1992
Bantam edition / June 1993*

ROAD TO AVONLEA is the trademark of Sullivan Films Inc.

*Skylark Books is a registered trademark of Bantam Books,
a division of Bantam Doubleday Dell Publishing Group, Inc.
Registered in U.S. Patent and Trademark Office and elsewhere.*

*All rights reserved.
Storybook written by Heather Conkie.
Copyright © 1992 by HarperCollins Publishers, Sullivan Films
Distribution, Inc., and Ruth Macdonald and David Macdonald.
No part of this book may be reproduced or transmitted in any form or by any means,
electronic or mechanical, including photocopying, recording, or by any information
storage and retrieval system, without permission in writing from the publisher.
For information address: HarperCollins Publishers Ltd., Suite 2900,
Hazelton Lanes, 55 Avenue Road, Toronto, Canada M5R 3L2.*

ISBN 0-553-48041-3

*Bantam Books are published by Bantam Books, a division of Bantam Doubleday Dell
Publishing Group, Inc. Its trademark, consisting of the words "Bantam Books" and the
portrayal of a rooster, is Registered in U.S. Patent and Trademark Office and in other
countries. Marca Registrada. Bantam Books, 1540 Broadway, New York, New York 10036.*

PRINTED IN THE UNITED STATES OF AMERICA
OPM   0 9 8 7 6 5 4 3 2 1

Chapter One

The wheels of the buggy traveled smartly along the winding country road. The sea was visible for just a moment, peeking between two grassy knolls of a gently rolling meadow with the path of the afternoon sun shining across its surface. Hetty King gave the reins a little flick and breathed in the fresh air with contentment. Beside her was Rachel Lynde, her hands folded neatly in her lap and her ample body swaying with the motion of the buggy. Tucked between the two of them was Hetty's niece, Sara Stanley. They were all dressed in their finest.

"Thank you for picking me up, Hetty," said Rachel, heartily. "What with Marilla leaving to visit Anne and all, I have no means of getting around."

"That's what friends are for, Rachel," said Hetty, pleasantly.

"Well, I'm forever grateful that we've settled our little quarrel," effused Rachel, looking as smug as a cat with butter on its paws.

Sara rolled her eyes. Little quarrel! It had been more like a thirty-year war! she thought to herself.

"Romney Penhallow certainly wasn't worth it," said Hetty emphatically, smiling across Sara at her friend as she steered the buggy across a little bridge.

"Come on Blackie! Up you go! That's a girl!" she called, and the old horse clattered across the wooden slats. Virginia creeper and periwinkle had grown over and around the ancient railing of the bridge. For a moment, the world around the three travelers was a blur of fresh, sweet green.

"I wouldn't miss this little party for anything," said Rachel above the clip-clop of the horse's hooves. "Can't wait to see what sort of a fellow that high-strung, simpering Alice Hardy finally managed to land. Mind you, she was in no position to be choosy. She was well on her way to becoming an old maid." She glanced quickly over Sara's head. "No offense, Hetty."

Sara exchanged a look with her aunt. Hetty's face remained pleasant, but stiff, mindful of the precarious nature of the newly revived friendship between Rachel and herself.

"Not everyone is cut out to be married, Rachel," she said crisply. "I, for one, enjoy the freedom that not being married provides."

Rachel Lynde was always one to call a spade a spade. She prided herself on it. As far as she was concerned, Hetty was not being exactly honest about the whole matter.

"Don't give me that malarkey, Hetty King!" She laughed. "You know as well as anyone, you were just terrified to take the leap!"

Sara could see that Aunt Hetty was having a hard time biting her tongue, but Rachel continued, oblivious, as usual, to anyone else's discomfort.

"Oh, it's all very well to talk about freedom till you're dreadful lonely in your old age." She nodded her head vigorously to accentuate her point, and the beige and brown silk flowers on her hat seemed perilously close to falling off.

"Well, you should know, Rachel," replied Hetty, smiling as she looked straight ahead up the road, enjoying the sweet taste of victory.

Sara tried hard to hide a giggle and ended up covering it with a coughing fit behind her hankie. Rachel frowned and shot a look at Hetty, not sure whether or not she was being insulted, but nothing in her friend's face betrayed her real meaning. Nevertheless, Rachel felt the need to set the record straight, no matter what Hetty King might or might not have meant.

"Just between you, me and the gatepost, Hetty, I always dreaded being a widow. But at least I have the freedom of the unmarried without having to put up with the awful stigma of being an old maid." She nodded for emphasis.

Sandwiched between the two, Sara put her hankie away and made a great effort to look with interest at the passing scenery. She couldn't help but feel a little responsible for the truce that her Aunt Hetty and Rachel Lynde had called to their longtime quarrel. After all, it had been Sara and her cousin, Felicity King, who had set the wheels in motion. If they hadn't kidnapped—well, perhaps *rescued* was a better word to use—that poor little orphan baby and left it on Malcolm and

Abigail McEwan's doorstep, Hetty and Rachel wouldn't have become the child's honorary god-mothers. And that, as everyone knew, was what had finally brought them back together after so many years of feuding.

However, peace among nations is rarely easy, and ever since the day the two women had finally decided to forgive and forget, they had circled each other carefully, each watching the other's every move, smiles dutifully in place.

Hetty was busy formulating a suitable reply to Rachel's last comment when, suddenly, their conversation was rudely interrupted by a sound completely and totally unfamiliar to any of them—except perhaps Sara.

Three lace-and-flower bedecked heads swiveled to locate the source of the remorseless din. It was a motorcar! A bright yellow motorcar! It approached them quickly from behind, its driver in goggles, his white scarf blowing in the wind. He beeped his horn loudly and passed them in a cloud of noise and dust. In doing so, he star-tled Blackie, and the buggy nearly went off the road.

"A motorcar! In Avonlea!" said Rachel, with as much disbelief as disgust.

Sara was entranced as she watched the beautiful shiny machine disappear over a hill ahead of them. "It's beautiful! It's just like the one we had in Montreal!"

"Of all the blasted, inconsiderate, reckless..." Hetty huffed. "I intend to find out who was driving that contraption if it's the last thing I do!"

Chapter Two

Alec King stood on the front lawn of the King Farm, smiling and greeting guests as they arrived at the engagement party he and his wife Janet were giving in honor of the bride-to-be, Alice Hardy. It was not his idea of how to spend a lovely, sunny, weekend afternoon, but Janet was a good friend of the bride's mother, and, well, once Janet made up her mind to do something...

He stuck his finger inside the stiff collar of his shirt and attempted to release its stranglehold on his neck. He sighed. Approaching him across the yard was Nathanial Hardy, hand outstretched heartily, smiling magnanimously. He could afford to smile, because he wasn't the one picking up the bill for this elegant affair, thought Alec, a little unkindly but accurately.

Nathanial Hardy was rich, and let everyone know it. He was also as tight as a vice-grip with a dollar. It was awkward to dislike the husband of one of his wife's best friends, but Alec couldn't help it. He winced as Nathanial's vice-grip pumped his hand up and down.

In Nathanial's wake stood his daughter, Alice, a timid, gangly young woman who always looked on the verge of tears. Alec supposed that the fellow beside her must be her fiancé, already an old man at twenty, too pompous and serious for his liking.

"Alec King," boomed Nathanial Hardy with the voice of a foghorn. "I'd like to present my future son-in-law, Edward P. Fraser—you can call him Teddy."

Alec smiled dutifully and shook the unfortunate young man's damp hand. "Good to meet you, Teddy. Welcome to the King Farm."

"So decent of you and Janet to throw this little party," said Nathanial, slapping him on the back. "Isn't it, Mother?"

Alec turned to see Mrs. Hardy, who had sidled up behind him, all mother-of-the-bride smiles.

"Oh, yes," she gushed. "Isn't it, Alice?"

Poor Alice seemed incapable of speech. Clutching her fiancé's arm, she nodded and smiled awkwardly.

"We have a surprise guest, Alec," continued Mrs. Hardy. "Teddy here has a famous uncle, who's just arrived out of the blue. We're so thrilled he could come. Hope you don't mind," she said excitedly.

She pointed in the direction of a man, dressed in white, who, along with a certain yellow motorcar, was the center of attention among a number of guests. There was something very familiar about the man. He had a certain courtly air, Alec thought, but he couldn't quite place him.

"Mind? Not at all!" Alec said, realizing that Mrs. Hardy was waiting for some sort of reply or statement of approval. He nodded towards the motorcar. "I'll have to have a closer look at that vehicle.... Now, if you'll excuse me, make yourselves at home, I must find Janet."

Alec shook a few more hands and escaped into the house.

Mr. and Mrs. Hardy threaded their way through the crowd to the dashing stranger and introduced themselves. Before the man could say anything, Nathanial took over the conversation.

"I must congratulate you, sir. I understand the Governor General himself hosted your art exhibition in Charlottetown. It's good to see a son of Avonlea getting his proper recognition."

The stranger looked at Mr. Hardy with thinly veiled amusement. His face was finely lined; a brown shock of hair fell over his forehead. He was still boyishly handsome for all his almost fifty years, and his sardonic smile made him seem even younger.

"You are very kind, Mr. Hardy, but I'd hardly call myself a 'son of Avonlea.' I've managed to avoid this place successfully for some thirty-odd years."

"Oh, you can't fool me, Mr. Penhallow," guffawed Mr. Hardy. "Once an Islander, always an Islander."

"Good Lord, I hope not!" said the stranger, coolly surveying the party guests over Mr. Hardy's head.

"Our Alice is simply thrilled you could come," cooed Mrs. Hardy, at her husband's side.

One dark eyebrow arched in amusement. "Is

she?" He smiled, disarmingly. "Charming girl. Exactly what my sister's boy deserves."

Whatever *double entendres* were intended were lost on Mrs. Hardy, who found, to her surprise, that her heart fluttered slightly in the presence of this stranger. She looked up at him coquettishly from beneath fluttering eyelashes, something she hadn't done for at least twenty-five years.

"It isn't everyday we get to meet a famous *artiste* such as yourself, let alone embrace him to our family bosom."

The man just stared at her, and then down at Mrs. Hardy's own very ample bosom.

"Let's not monopolize our guest, Mother," blustered Mr. Hardy. "Come, I'll introduce you to some old acquaintances."

"Thank you," said the man, with a little bow. "I can hardly wait."

Mrs. Hardy smiled helplessly as her husband led him away.

Hetty King was still bristling with anger as she drove up to the yard. Suddenly, Sara stood up, pointing, and almost knocked poor Rachel out of the buggy.

"There's the motorcar, Aunt Hetty!" And there it was, large as life, parked under the apple trees.

Hetty's eyes glinted with pleasure. "Well, well, I'm in luck. Whoever owns that hideous machine will soon get a piece of my mind."

Their arrival had not gone unnoticed. Teddy Fraser's famous uncle, still surrounded by a group of admirers, looked with interest as Hetty, Rachel and Sara walked towards the house and began to mingle with the guests. He watched as Mrs. Hardy made a beeline for Hetty.

"Hetty, where is Olivia?" she asked, before Hetty could even say "hello" or "how are you?" "Don't tell me she wasn't able to come!" the woman whined.

"I'm afraid not, Mrs. Hardy," replied Hetty tersely, her mind on other, more pressing things—such as who was responsible for almost putting her buggy in the ditch! "She's off gallivanting. Something to do with that newspaper."

"How sad," moaned Mrs. Hardy. "I was hoping she might give our little get-together a few lines in her social column."

The man gazed fixedly at Hetty.

"You remember Clara Potts?" Mr. Hardy's

booming voice interrupted his thoughts. He turned to the broadly smiling woman at his elbow.

"Clara...Potts, is it now? How good to see you again," he said, reaching down and giving her hand a kiss.

Mrs. Potts could hardly contain herself. "Of course. It's been such a long time," she gushed, her face going the color of her crimson-feathered hat.

A very thirsty Rachel was heading for the tea table when she spotted the man in the white suit talking to Clara Potts. She stopped in her tracks; her eyes narrowed. She prided herself on never forgetting a face, and, for a second, she was quite shocked when she recognized this one. She soon recovered herself, however, and lost no time in crossing the lawn towards the pair. Not one to stand on ceremony, Rachel thrust out her gloved hand and smiled broadly up at the handsome face.

"Hello there! I recognize you, I think, from a long time ago."

The man stared back at her, recognition dawning slowly. He kissed the extended hand.

"How could I forget you...Rachel...Rachel...

I've never been good with last names...but you haven't changed really...."

"How wonderful!" exclaimed a beaming Rachel. "You must have a very good memory! I'm Rachel Lynde now. I married Thomas Lynde, God rest his soul."

"We were just saying, Rachel," purred Clara Potts, "how Hetty King and this gentleman were beaux once upon a time."

"They were—until I broke it up, Clara," burst out Rachel, hooting and poking the poor man in the ribs.

But he didn't reply. He was once again watching Hetty as she made her way among the guests on the lawn.

"Why, the moron almost put us into the ditch. It was all I could do to control the horse!"

Alice Hardy stood listening, white-faced. The bride-to-be was the first person Hetty found at the party to tell her complaints to.

"I'm dreadfully sorry, Miss King, but I'm sure my fiancé's uncle didn't mean to cause you any alarm," she squeaked nervously, more than a little intimidated by Hetty's wrath.

"And who is your fiancé, my dear?" asked

Hetty, bluntly. "I haven't had the pleasure as yet. Let's hope he has more sense than his uncle."

Alice motioned frantically to her young man, who hastened to her assistance.

"Miss King, I'd like you to meet my fiancé, Edward P. Fraser."

Hetty held out her hand. "And what does the 'P' stand for?" she asked.

"Penhallow, ma'am," he replied stiffly. "My mother's maiden name."

Hetty smiled rigidly. "I once knew a Penhallow. Not that I will hold it against you."

Clara Potts's corset was threatening to burst as she held her sides with mirth.

"Oh, I can still remember the most terrible practical jokes you and Hetty used to play on one another. Like the time Hetty put the dead seagull in your lunch bucket!"

Both Clara and Rachel exploded into very unladylike guffaws.

"Oh no, Clara!" gasped Rachel. "The pig's eye in the pencil case was far better than that!"

The two women dissolved once again into peals of laughter. Oblivious to their carryings-on,

Teddy P. Fraser's uncle continued to smile politely.

Rachel came to her senses first and followed his gaze to where Hetty stood, talking to the milquetoast fiancé of Alice Hardy. Rachel squinted her eyes at the man beside her and then darted a look at Hetty. He was watching Hetty King, no doubt about it.

Mrs. Potts had observed this as well, and the women's eyes met. A decision was silently made. Giggling nervously, both Mrs. Potts and Rachel excused themselves and made a beeline for an unsuspecting Hetty as she took her leave of a relieved Alice Hardy, still clutching her fiancé's arm, and made her way to the tea table.

Rachel approached Hetty with a smirk on her face, Clara Potts close behind her.

"Hetty, do you know who that man is over there?" Rachel asked coyly, gesturing towards the tall stranger in white.

"What man, Rachel?" asked Hetty, intent on keeping her teacup balanced while she bit into a sugar cookie.

Sara, who was making a difficult decision among all the sweets at the tea table, looked over to the garden where the man stood, sipping tea and calmly staring back at them.

"The one in white, Aunt Hetty," Sara said. "The one who was driving the motorcar. He's staring right at you."

Hetty's eyes lit up. "Oh, so *he's* the one, is he? Good! Because I intend to tell him a thing or two!"

Hetty, on the warpath, advanced towards the man with Sara and the two women close behind. Rachel and Clara Potts exchanged delighted looks.

"I should have known," Hetty sniffed. "Look at the supercilious look on his face. I know he's Alice Hardy's fiancé's uncle, but what's his name?"

"Romney!" said Rachel, gleefully.

Hetty halted, and Sara could have sworn that the color not only drained away from her face, but the pink roses in her hat seemed to visibly wilt.

"Romney...?" she repeated nervously, her voice barely audible.

"Romney Penhallow!" pronounced Mrs. Potts, and she was not disappointed when she saw the effect that name had on Hetty.

Chapter Three

Hetty's teacup started rattling against its saucer. "Oh, good Lord!" was all she uttered. She turned to make a hasty retreat, but the women blocked her way.

"You'll have to admit, his looks have improved with age," said Rachel appraisingly. "Looks like he didn't go bald after all!"

Mrs. Potts yanked at Hetty's elbow. "Come and say hello, Hetty. He's a famous artist now. He's traveled all over the world!"

Hetty looked nervously over her shoulder at the man still watching calmly from the garden. Their eyes met, and she immediately averted her gaze.

"I wouldn't care if he was the King of England!" said Hetty, her voice strangled. "I vowed in seventh grade never to speak to him again, and I intend to keep my word."

Rachel was incredulous. "I thought we'd put all that behind us, Hetty King. That was thirty years ago!"

"It will be thirty-six years this coming Christmas," stated Hetty flatly.

Rachel shook her head. "I can't fathom your attitude."

Mrs. Potts leaned forward, her eyes twinkling. "Don't you agree, Rachel, that it's time she learned to let bygones be bygones?"

"I certainly do!" said Rachel emphatically. "Come along, Hetty. Now don't be shy!"

With that, Rachel took one of Hetty's arms and Mrs. Potts took the other and they began to lead, or rather drag, Hetty towards Romney Penhallow. Sara followed behind, thrilled that she would meet, at last, the man who had been the cause of the thirty-year war!

Hetty was beside herself. "Rachel Lynde," she hissed, "if you value my friendship...don't you dare..."

Romney's smile was more sardonic than usual as he watched, with great amusement, Hetty being led towards him.

"Please...don't! Just leave it alone!" Hetty pleaded with the two women in a harsh whisper, though in vain.

Rachel gave her a little push forward and there she was, face to face with Romney Penhallow.

Rachel smiled at him, her eyes twinkling. "There is someone here I thought you'd want to renew old acquaintance with," she said, with a slight nudge and a wink.

"Good heavens!" he said with a big smile, feigning surprise. "It's Hetty King. My, it's been a long time! Romney Penhallow." He extended his hand, but Hetty ignored the gesture completely, her eyes flitting about desperately for some avenue of escape.

Sara tugged at her aunt's sleeve. "Aunt Hetty!" she said pleadingly, but Hetty had no intention of breaking her word and talking to this man. The silence between the two was deafening, and Rachel, above all else, hated silence.

"I'm afraid Hetty has become...somewhat hard of hearing," said Rachel, raising her voice to a shout, delighting in Hetty's reaction to this fib.

Mrs. Potts barely managed to suppress a snort of laughter. Romney tried to look very sympathetic as Hetty fumed in frustration.

Rachel couldn't resist gilding the lily. "In fact, *very* hard of hearing," she added. "Deaf!"

Sara's eyes lit up as she caught on to the joke. "It happened quite suddenly...overnight," she piped up, quite liking the crinkles at the corners of this man's eyes. Here was someone who obviously loved to laugh.

Hetty stared at Sara, not believing her own niece could be so brazen as to poke fun at her in her misery!

Mrs. Potts, of course, couldn't resist adding her two cents' worth. "Such an affliction for my dear friend, and barely into her golden years."

"Well, I can't see why it would make much of a difference," said Romney, quickly. "She never did listen to anyone else anyway."

Rachel Lynde and Clara Potts hooted with laughter. This was too much!

Hetty had taken a swallow of her tea for something to do and almost choked on it. Other guests had become aware of the little confrontation going on in their midst and necks began to crane. Hetty noticed the sudden silence around them and stared malevolently at her two friends, daring them with her eyes to go any further. But they were not to be stopped. Rachel took the ball and kept it rolling.

"It's made her go quite peculiar," she chortled. "You never know *what* she might do next!"

"Then I guess she hasn't changed at all!" said Romney blithely, and once again the two women went into gales of laughter, only this time they were joined by some of the guests closest to the action.

A shade of red started creeping up Hetty's neck to the top of her cheekbones. Never in all her life had she felt so angry and humiliated. She took what she hoped was one last, defiant look at that sardonic smile, slammed down her teacup, spilling its contents, and walked away in as dignified a manner as she could muster.

Sara, Rachel and Clara Potts exchanged surprised glances. The guests looked at each other with raised eyebrows. The ones in the know murmured and laughed. Those who were too far away to have witnessed the scene were completely bewildered. Everyone watched as Hetty marched across the lawn and climbed into her buggy.

"What in heaven's name...?" said an astonished Mrs. Hardy. "She just got here!"

Romney Penhallow paused only a second and then headed for his car.

"Hetty! Where are you going?" called Mrs. Hardy as Hetty and her buggy disappeared down the driveway.

Romney turned the crank on his car and it came to life with a roar. He hopped into it nimbly and steered it down the road after the buggy.

The crowd buzzed as speculation, rumor and gossip ran through it like wildfire.

The noise of the motorcar took Mr. Hardy's attention away from a cream cake he was busy devouring. "What on earth is going on?" he sputtered, hoping that his honored guest wasn't leaving so soon.

Alec King came out of the house to see half the guests running down his driveway, following the racket of the motorcar. "What the...? Janet!" he called and disappeared back in the house.

Romney waved gaily to the crowd as they fell further and further behind.

Chapter Four

One of the ribbons on her hat had come undone and was trailing in the breeze behind her, but a furious Hetty didn't care. All she wanted to do was go home, though an infernal racket behind her told her that it wasn't going to be that easy. She looked over her shoulder to see Romney gaining on her at a quick rate. She urged Blackie to go faster, but the poor animal was no match for this shining piece of machinery. Slowly, Hetty's anger was replaced with an unexpected excitement. She had forgotten how she liked a chase. Her competitive spirit soared, and as Blackie picked up speed, she thought, for a brief second, she might win.

But the noise got closer and closer, and finally, when she turned, it was to see Romney driving up alongside her. He beeped his horn, smiling broadly.

"Come on now, Hetty King! Don't be so darned stubborn! Talk to me!"

The brazen, blasted nerve of the man! thought Hetty.

"I'm flattered," he called out, smiling his infuriating smile. "I hardly expected you'd remember me, let alone still bear a grudge."

Hetty spurred Blackie on, not giving an inch. The one-lane bridge loomed ahead of them and they approached it neck-and-neck, each of them determined to get there first and neither willing to give way.

"Come now! Talk to me!" he called.

Hetty still refused to answer, and suddenly the motorcar accelerated with a burst of speed and passed her in a cloud of dust. She watched, incredulous and with gritted teeth, as Romney swerved the car around and brought it to a stop, directly across the middle of the bridge, blocking her way.

Hetty pulled frantically on the reins and poor Blackie came to a halt just in time, neighing and fighting against the traces.

Romney hopped neatly and calmly out of the car and walked towards her. The horse was startled again as the car backfired belatedly.

"Whoa, whoa there!" he said soothingly, and Blackie tossed her mane with outraged dignity.

Hetty, on the other hand, had lost all semblance of decorum as she clambered across the buggy seat, retreating to the other side with alarm. Her hat was perched at a very odd angle and she glared at Romney from under its brim as he approached.

"Perhaps now you'll speak to me," he said, smiling up at her unperturbed. He extended his hand to help her out of the buggy, but Hetty would have none of it and attempted to climb out the opposite side—the side facing the river. She misjudged how close she really was to the river bank and, instead of hitting firm ground when she climbed from the buggy, her foot felt nothing but thin air. A scream escaped her lips as she fell directly into the river.

The only other person as surprised as Hetty was Romney. He ran around the buggy just in time to see her come sputtering to the surface.

The more curious of the crowd from the party had by this time caught up with the chase, and they felt well rewarded for their hard run. Few could resist giggling at the most uncommon sight of Hetty King taking a dunking.

Romney removed his jacket and rushed along the riverbank. Hetty was trying desperately to keep her balance, but her waterlogged lace dress kept pulling her down into the shallow river.

Sara and Rachel arrived, out of breath, and stood watching, open-mouthed.

"Aunt Hetty!" Sara cried, and then, spying Romney, shouted, "Mr. Penhallow, help her!"

"Don't worry," he called back. "I'll save her!"

"You...*idiot*!" Hetty shrieked as Romney reached the edge of the river.

Romney grinned. "She speaks! It's a miracle!" he proclaimed, as he chivalrously jumped into the water.

"You must be drunk!" Hetty snapped at him as he waded towards her, up to his waist in muddy river water.

"On this godforsaken island of temperance? Hardly likely!" he shot back, his brown hair falling in his eyes. Still wearing a broad grin, he reached out to take her hand. Hetty accepted it and then very deliberately gave it a yank, so that he too fell face first into the water.

The crowd on the bank broke into hearty laughter at these antics.

Romney, still smiling, awkwardly regained his balance, but as he did so, he mistakenly stepped on the skirt of Hetty's dress as she struggled to get out of the water.

"Get off my skirt!" she yelled. "You're standing on my blasted hem!"

It was too late. He stumbled again, and the seams of the skirt gave way. Unaware that her skirt remained behind, pinned by Romney's foot, a determined Hetty waded through the water to the shore, her shoes sticking in the muddy bottom. She pulled herself out by gripping the reeds along the side of the bank, and only when she heard another shriek of laughter from the onlookers did she realize that all she was wearing were her long knickers.

Romney slogged over towards her.

"Don't you dare come near me!" she hissed at him.

He reached back into the water and handed her her skirt. "You might need this!" he said with a grin.

The group along the riverbank applauded wildly. Hetty grabbed the muddy, drenched remains of her skirt, and, throwing a baleful look at him, she strutted up the road in her knickers, trying vainly to wrap the soaking garment around herself, accompanied by the laughs and merriment of the delighted spectators. Who would have thought that Alice Hardy's engagement party would turn out to be such a hilarious occasion?

Romney stood, shaking his head and chuckling, as he, too, watched Hetty make her way up the road.

Chapter Five

The lamps were lit in the cozy Rose Cottage kitchen as Olivia King cleared away the remains of dinner. Sara was busy washing the dishes and telling her Aunt Olivia the story of the after-noon's events when Alec King came in the back door and dropped a load of wood by the old stove.

"...and there was Aunt Hetty..." Sara said in a hushed voice, "...striding down the road, with hardly a stitch on!" She giggled and covered her mouth with her hand.

Olivia chuckled in spite of herself. "Oh Sara, I can hardly believe it...poor Hetty!" She looked down at Hetty's empty plate at the end of the table and shook her head. "I guess I'll keep things warm in case she decides she wants to eat something later."

Alec shook his head with amusement and brushed the bark from his hands into the open grate.

"Well, well. Hetty and Romney Penhallow at it again after all these years. I knew there was something familiar about the fellow. I just couldn't place him."

In the darkening hallway, halfway down the stairs, Hetty King stood clutching her hankie. She could hear their low tones and suppressed laughter, and she crept closer to the kitchen door to listen.

"Were they really beaux, Uncle Alec?" asked Sara. "Rachel Lynde said they were madly in love."

Hetty's eyebrows shot up, and she suppressed a sneeze just in time to prevent her discovery.

Alec shook his head. "Well, if they were, they sure had an odd way of showing it. Thick as thieves one minute and plotting against each other the next."

"But why did they stop speaking to each other in the first place?" asked Sara, putting away the last of the plates. It was something she had always wondered about and had never been able to coax her Aunt Hetty into divulging.

Alec frowned as he tried to remember. "I think Romney Penhallow asked Rachel Lynde to the Avonlea Christmas party, just to make Hetty jealous. But it backfired. Hetty swore she would never speak to either of them again."

"And we all know Hetty," said Olivia. "Look how long it took her to give in and speak to Rachel Lynde."

"Poor old Romney begged her forgiveness, but Hetty wouldn't budge an inch. Seems to me, it was soon after that he left the Island."

Sara looked dreamily out the window to where the moon was throwing dapples of light on the lawn and garden. "It's so romantic," she sighed. "Maybe he's come back to stay."

"Perhaps," said Olivia, but she giggled when she caught sight of Alec's face, his eyes raised to heaven.

Hetty had had enough. She walked purposefully through the kitchen door.

"I heard the bunch of you buzzing away in here. No doubt that's what everyone else in Avonlea is doing at this very moment, thanks to Rachel Lynde." She picked up a teacup and filled it from the teapot on the stove.

Alec cleared his throat. "Hetty, don't you think you're making too much of a fuss?"

Hetty wheeled around and faced her brother indignantly. "I'm making too much of a fuss? I nearly drown in the river, I nearly break my neck! The whole town's laughing at me...and I'm making too much of a fuss?!"

"You have to admit, it was funny, Aunt Hetty," began Sara, but her aunt fixed her with a steely glare. "I mean...not that you might have been hurt...but it was funny when your skirt came off...." Sara finished lamely.

Olivia lost her battle with a fit of giggles and buried her face in a tea towel.

"Oh...I didn't hear that part!" said Alec, and he started to chuckle, though he immediately turned to busy himself with stacking the wood-pile more symmetrically.

Sara bit her bottom lip, but the laughter was infectious, and soon she too was doubled over.

Hetty would cheerfully have throttled the lot of them, but instead she merely stared at their display of mirth with a baleful eye.

Olivia was the first to recover herself. She noticed that behind her sister's haughty glare there were some genuinely hurt feelings.

"Oh now, Hetty, we're only teasing," she said gently, still stifling the urge to giggle. "I'm sure that by tomorrow everyone will have forgotten about the incident."

Olivia really meant it, but somehow her words weren't very convincing.

Chapter Six

In many larger villages, Olivia's prediction would have come true. Life would have continued on in its normal way, one day's entertainment forgotten in the midst of other interesting occurrences and anecdotes to tell. But Avonlea was simply too small for that to happen. And so it was that when Hetty King arrived in town to do her regular daily shopping, she became increasingly, uncomfortably aware of clusters of townsfolk tittering and laughing behind their hands when she walked by.

As she approached the general store, she spied a group of children she recognized from her classroom drawing on a white picket fence. As she drew closer, they shushed each other and started to giggle. Hetty's eyes flew open as she gazed at a picture they had drawn crudely on the fence. It was a picture of her in her knickers, dripping with water. "MISS KING IN HER NICKERS," someone had written beside it in huge, ungainly letters with a piece of charcoal. Hetty was shaken at the sight, but instantly realized that she mustn't, at all costs, let her feelings show. That would be the end of any control she might have in the classroom.

She straightened her back and strode over to the children, whose smiles were already wiped off their faces. She walked right up to one unfortunate little freckle-faced girl and took the offending piece of charcoal from her.

She then strutted to the fence and, with a flourish, she added a "K" to the beginning of the word "nickers."

"I can see we'll have to spend more time on your spelling lessons, Mathilda Blewett," she said to the surprised child, handing her back the charcoal. She then brushed the black dust from her hands and strode away.

The children looked at her with a mixture of surprise and new respect. One boy started to giggle nervously, but a look from his friends was enough to silence him.

Hetty continued on her way, not nearly as self-possessed as she had just appeared to be. She gritted her teeth as the undeniable sound of Romney's car backfiring reached her ears from down the street. Suddenly, the offending piece of machinery appeared, or rather careened around the corner near the blacksmith's shop. Chickens scattered and older ladies jumped as he tooted his horn at them.

Hetty walked with great purpose, head high and eyes forward, but the man had no intention of letting her pass. His brakes squealed as the car came to a stop beside her and, standing up in his car, he executed an exaggerated bow.

"I hardly recognize you when you're dry!" he called.

"I hardly recognize you when you're sober!" Hetty shot back, surprising even herself that such words could possibly come out of her mouth.

Romney was far from insulted. In fact, he exploded with laughter. "*Touché*!" he yelled, mock saluting her. "You always could dish it out, Hetty King!"

An infinitesimal twitch at the side of Hetty's mouth betrayed a smile, but she fled towards the general store.

"It's as plain as the nose on your face that she still has some feelings for him, and he for her! And do you want to know what I think? She's fooling herself if she doesn't admit it!"

Mrs. Potts waggled her finger up and down and nodded her head emphatically at Mrs. Lawson, who had listened, spellbound, to that lady's colorful description of the goings-on at Alice Hardy's party.

The bell over the front door of the general store tinkled; Mrs. Lawson threw a warning glance at Clara Potts and tipped her head towards the door.

Hetty entered quickly, almost furtively, and stood for a second staring back out into the street.

"Hello, Hetty," chirped Mrs. Potts in a singsong voice.

Hetty jumped and turned from the window.

"Oh, Hetty, your hat's arrived!" said Mrs. Lawson, glad to be busy with something, knowing full well that Hetty's ears must be burning.

Mrs. Potts beamed knowingly at Hetty as she approached the counter. "That was quite the show you and Romney provided us with yesterday. I haven't laughed so much since Pat Frewen's pig took a run at Reverend Leonard."

Mrs. Potts was always her own best audience, and she broke into gales of laughter. A stifled, giggling sound came from the direction of the ladder on which Mrs. Lawson perched as she pulled a box down from one of the shelves.

Hetty's cheeks went pink and her eyes narrowed with embarrassed fury. "You have your nerve even speaking to me, Clara Potts, after all the grief you've caused."

Mrs. Potts raised her eyebrows to her hat brim. "I've caused!" she said in self-righteous shock. "You're the one who made a circus of the whole affair! All you had to do was be civil to Romney in the first place and none of this would ever have happened!"

Hetty looked the woman straight in the eye. "You and Rachel Lynde! You're two of a kind! Both of you are cut from the same cloth!" She turned on her heel and headed towards the door.

"Hetty?" called Mrs. Lawson meekly.

Hetty swung around, her eyes still blazing.

"Your hat..." she finished, uncomfortably. Mrs. Lawson did not like conflict of any kind, especially in her store.

Hetty whisked back and snatched the hat box. Once again she puffed herself up at Clara Potts. "A pair of vicious, interfering meddlers! That's what you are!"

With that, she turned and strode out of the store, letting the door bang loudly behind her.

"Oh dear," said Mrs. Lawson.

Mrs. Potts looked innocently dumfounded. "Now doesn't that beat all? If Hetty King were a dog, she'd bite the hand that fed her. Well, I suppose we're all as the Lord made us!"

At the other end of town, in the office of the Avonlea *Chronicle*, above the post office,

Olivia King was waiting patiently for her editor to finish reading an article she had just submitted.

She was feeling proud of herself. It had taken some doing, but she had managed to convince the premier of Prince Edward Island to give her an interview. She had traveled all the way to Summerside, where he was opening a county fair, in the hopes of getting a few minutes to talk to him. Even though she'd missed what had certainly turned out to be a very eventful party, it had been worth it. The premier had been charming, and had divulged to her more opinions on the pressing issues of the day than he'd offered to even the most seasoned reporters from the Charlottetown papers.

Mr. Tyler put the sheets of paper down on his desk and pushed them towards Olivia. "It's a fine interview, Olivia, but I doubt if there will be a paper to print it in."

Olivia, nonplussed, rose to her feet. Was the man joking?

"I beg your pardon, Mr. Tyler?"

Her editor rubbed his forehead wearily. "I've decided that it's time to shut the newspaper down."

Olivia looked at him in disbelief and sank into the chair opposite. "But why? I don't understand."

Mr. Tyler, looking much older than his years, got up and slowly walked over to a shelf, his shoulders slumped. He shuffled through some papers and then handed a page to Olivia. "The Carmody newspaper has systematically stolen all my top advertisers."

Olivia studied the sheet of paper, her brow furrowed. "How?"

"By undercutting my prices," he replied flatly. "Nathanial Hardy's Steamship Company was the first to go, and all the rest have followed. I'm sorry, Olivia, but I can't see that there's any point in carrying on. I've made up my mind to take my small inheritance and invest it in a more lucrative venture." He sat down again, his chin resting on his folded hands.

Olivia stared at him. He was serious! But her mind was racing. This couldn't happen. She wouldn't let it happen. There *must* be a solution. She looked at the numbers on the sheet in her hands—prices for advertising in the Carmody paper. Just glancing at it, she could see how much lower they were than the *Chronicle*'s. No wonder they were losing business.

"Why can't you match their prices?" she asked. "Why don't we just lower our rates?"

Mr. Tyler smiled at her in that irritating, patronizing way that could make her blood boil. "I can't afford to," he answered simply.

"But the readership is up," Olivia persisted.

"But it's advertising that keeps the paper alive, and without it we're dead," he replied, as if he were speaking to a child. "I'm sorry, Olivia."

How dare he give up so easily? Olivia thought to herself. She, for one, wasn't about to. She snatched up her article from the desk, straightened her back and lifted her chin.

"Mr. Tyler," she said, her eyes flashing with determination, "I intend to have this printed, and in this paper."

Chapter Seven

The soothing murmur of the crickets and the distant rumble of the sea did nothing to calm the troubled waters in Hetty King's soul as she stood leaning against the porch railing of Rose Cottage, looking morosely out into the dark. All her life she had strived to be looked upon with respect. She had struggled to go to teacher's college—the only girl from her class to have done so. She had emerged from that institution with honors, and as a result she had returned to become the revered schoolmistress of the Avonlea School. She considered herself to be an upstanding citizen with a fine family background and ancestral roots that ran deep into the soil of the Island. And now, in just one day, all that had been taken away from her. All that she had ever held dear—the respect of her family, her students, her village—had disappeared. All because of that devil, Romney Penhallow! She took a deep breath and went inside.

Olivia and Sara were busy working on a dress pattern on the oval table in the parlor. Sara looked up at her Aunt Olivia's face, flushed in the light of the lamp.

"And you worked so hard to get the interview with Premier Mackenzie," she said sympathetically, carefully pinning the thin pattern to the silky material.

Olivia pricked herself for the tenth time and angrily tried to concentrate on the task at hand. "I tell you Sara, I'm just at my wits' end with Mr. Tyler, but I'm not about to let him close down the Avonlea *Chronicle*."

Hetty emerged from the shadows of the hallway and paced the parlor, totally at loose ends. "I'm really not in the mood to listen to your little problems, Olivia," she said. "I have enough of my own."

Olivia and Sara exchanged a look.

"At least you're not the laughingstock of Avonlea," Hetty continued, crossing back and forth and wringing her hands. "I don't see how I can ever show my face again."

Sara felt sorry for her Aunt Hetty, but she couldn't think of anything to say that would make her feel better, so she turned her attention to Olivia's problem. That, at least, they might be able to do something about!

"Why don't you take over the paper yourself?" she asked.

Olivia smiled but shook her head. "Oh Sara, I don't have the experience or the resources. I could never do that."

"But I have some money, if you need it. I could simply write to Nanny Louisa," Sara insisted.

Olivia gave her shoulder a squeeze. "It's not the money, Sara, it's me. I just don't know if I could actually run it by myself."

"One thing I do know," came Hetty's gloomy voice from the shadows. "If you have any doubts about anything, don't do it. Remember that, Sara. I had great misgivings about going to the Hardy affair, come to think of it. I should have trusted my instincts and not gone." She continued to pace fretfully.

Olivia looked at her older sister and sighed. "If you listened to every doubt you ever had, Hetty, you'd never do anything."

"Yes, well, you don't have a head for business, Olivia. You never did," was Hetty's abrupt answer.

Olivia sucked in her breath in annoyance. There was that patronizing tone of voice again. She had heard enough of it in one day to last her a lifetime.

"You should just stick to telling your little stories," Hetty continued with a dismissive wave of her hand, unmindful of her sister's pent-up fury.

Olivia rose from her chair and strode towards Hetty. "I do not call an interview with the premier of this province a little story, Hetty!" she said icily.

Hetty was so involved in her own self-pity that she was caught quite off guard.

"And if Mr. Tyler had taken care of his business, the newspaper wouldn't be in this position right now!" Olivia continued, the sudden clarity of her thoughts surprising even her. "And if I were him, I would go to every single one of those advertisers and explain to them that their disloyalty is threatening the very life of the Avonlea *Chronicle*!" She finished to find both Sara and Hetty staring at her in surprise at her sudden, impassioned speech.

"Why don't you?" suggested Sara quietly after a moment's silence.

Hetty looked at Olivia with thinly veiled skepticism. Olivia caught the look and made a decision.

Taking a deep breath, she said, "Do you know what, Sara Stanley? I think I will. I'll see Nathanial Hardy tomorrow, at his daughter's wedding. I'll just go right up to him and...and explain the matter to him as plainly as I can!"

Sara hugged her aunt, who had sounded a lot more confident than she felt.

Hetty watched the two of them with a doubtful eye. "Take my word for it, you're setting yourself up for a fall," she warned.

Olivia rolled her eyes at such pessimism.

"Nothing ventured, Hetty, nothing gained!"

"My father used to always say, the bigger the risk, the bigger the rewards," Sara chipped in.

Hetty gave her niece a dark look. "The bigger the risk, Sara," she said severely, "the bigger the fool you look when you fail!"

"The true fool is someone who never takes risks!" Olivia blurted out.

Hetty looked away, not meeting her sister's eyes, and Olivia continued, close to tears.

"Oh Hetty, don't you see?" she asked quietly. "You're a teacher and you love it. You've done what you wanted to do with your life."

Hetty said nothing, but a look of intense sadness passed over her face, unobserved by her sister and niece standing as she was in the shadows beyond the lamplight.

Olivia's voice reached her from across the room.

"The newspaper gives me a chance to do something with mine."

The inhabitants of Rose Cottage retired early that evening. The comfort of eiderdown quilts was far preferable to the troubled silence that so often follows any sort of unresolved clash of opinions.

But not all the souls of Avonlea were keeping the same hours. Rounding the bend in the road that led to Rose Cottage, bustling along by the light of the moon, were Rachel Lynde and Clara Potts, their voices in competition with the chatter of the crickets.

"She called us interfering meddlers," huffed Mrs. Potts, trying her best to keep up with Rachel's long stride.

"Well," said Rachel decisively, "if that's what it takes, Clara!"

The two marched up the steps of the Rose Cottage porch and knocked smartly at the door, unmindful of the fact that there wasn't a lamp lit in any of the windows.

Olivia heard the knock first. She hadn't been able to sleep, worrying about the decision she had made so hurriedly and unexpectedly. She leaped out of bed and grabbed for her dressing gown, wondering who on earth could be paying them a visit at this time of night. As she passed Hetty's door, she heard the bedsprings creak and realized that Hetty, too, must be getting out of bed to investigate.

Olivia opened the door to find Rachel Lynde standing there, her hair put up as though she were about to go to bed and a shawl wrapped around her. Beside her was Clara Potts. Rachel smiled as if there was nothing unusual about a late-night visit and moved her bulk into the doorway.

"I am sorry to disturb you, Olivia. I am not in the habit of gallivanting around the town in the middle of the night, but I...well, at least Clara and I...couldn't let another day go by..."

Hetty, looking slightly out of character in a nightcap, appeared beside Olivia and attempted to close the door in Rachel's face. The determined Rachel jammed her foot in the door.

"Hetty!" she protested. "Please!"

Hetty looked at her through the crack in the door and opened it just slightly.

Mrs. Potts stepped forward from the shadows. "We're sorry to disturb you, Hetty, but Rachel and I couldn't let another day go by without—"

Rachel cut her off. "Thomas and I always made it a point to settle our disputes before bedtime," she said, matter-of-factly.

"The poor man probably died from lack of sleep!" snapped Hetty. "What are you doing here?"

"We've come to apologize," said Mrs. Potts, her voice as sweet as treacle.

"Before this escalates into another thirty-year war!" added Rachel. "Now we all know that Clara's tongue is hinged in the middle..."

Clara Potts' mouth dropped open and snapped shut just as quickly.

"...but if the truth be known," continued Rachel, "I couldn't bear the idea of you going to that wedding tomorrow and saying goodness knows what about me behind my back."

"You needn't have worried yourself, Rachel," said Hetty coldly. "I have no intention of going to that wedding."

Olivia looked at Hetty in surprise. "What? Of course you're going!"

Mrs. Potts was dumfounded. "What do you mean you're not going?" she asked bluntly.

"I have made up my mind, and that is that," said Hetty, dismissing them and attempting once again to close the door. "Now go home, both of you, and stay out of my affairs. Let us at least get some sleep!"

Rachel knew Hetty inside out, and what she didn't know for sure, she knew by intuition. Rachel prided herself on her intuition. She knew immediately what tack to take.

"Well!" she said mockingly as Hetty pressed

her weight against the door. "I never thought I'd see the day that Romney Penhallow would get the best of you. I'm amazed. You're getting old, Hetty, that's what!"

"You're losing your touch, Hetty! You are indeed!" Mrs. Potts chimed in.

Hetty let go of the door abruptly, her face a mask. "Thank you, ladies, for your capricious assessment. Good night!"

She turned and went up the stairs, leaving Olivia and the two night visitors to sigh and shrug their shoulders.

Hetty could hear the front door finally shut and Olivia's soft footfalls as she came up the stairs to bed. The glow of lamplight passed by the crack at the bottom of her door and then disappeared.

By the light of her own small dresser lamp, Hetty stood dejectedly in front of her mirror. She took off the nightcap and tentatively patted her hair, peering at her image. Her new hat lay on the dresser, and on impulse she picked it up and settled it on her head, looking at it critically. An old photograph of herself as a bright-eyed girl smiled up at her from the dresser top. She gazed at it sadly for a moment and then put it away in a drawer.

Chapter Eight

The morning of Alice Hardy's wedding dawned with bright promise. The sun streaked through the trees around Rose Cottage, dappling the ground with a golden light and sparkling on the dewy freshness of the climbing roses that gave the cottage its name.

Peter Craig, Hetty and Olivia's hired boy, whistled to himself as he hitched Blackie to the buggy. A whole day off, he thought to himself. He hadn't decided whether to go for a hike along the coast and look for clams or to go fishing with Felix King. Then he remembered that Felix was probably going to the Hardy wedding too, and he settled on the hike.

His thoughts were interrupted when Olivia came outside onto the front porch. Peter looked at her admiringly. She was absolutely beautiful in a dress of dotted swiss in pale lilac, trimmed with tiny seed pearls. Not that Peter noticed the color or the seed pearls. She just plain looked nice to him.

"Hurry, Sara," Olivia called back. "We don't want to be late."

The door opened and slammed shut and Sara hurried out. Peter whistled appreciatively at her appearance in her white eyelet-lace dress and matching hat.

Sara was not displeased by his reaction, but she felt it her duty to put him in his place.

"Peter Craig, it is the height of rudeness to whistle at a lady. I should think you'd know better."

Peter shook his head. Sara better watch herself, he thought. For a moment she sounded just like her Aunt Hetty.

Sara was extending her hand for Peter to help her into the buggy when suddenly Hetty herself made a grand entrance onto the porch. Olivia and Sara turned and stared at her. After what she'd said the night before, neither had expected her to be coming with them. But now here she was, looking quite stately and attractive and definitely dressed for a wedding. She had taken greater care than usual with her wardrobe and hair, and a shawl and new hat provided the crowning touch. No one said anything. Sara forgot her own rules of etiquette and whistled.

Hetty laughed nervously, obviously enjoying the effect she was having on them all. "Don't stand there gawking. We'll be late for the wedding," she said, taking Peter's arm as he helped her into the buggy.

Olivia and Sara exchanged a look of surprise, then Olivia gave the reins a little twitch and off they went, leaving Peter waving, his feet itching to get to the beach.

The White Sands Hotel was an impressive establishment, with its symmetrical gables and turrets rising majestically to the sky, its impeccable green lawns sloping down to the crystal blue of the ocean. It was the perfect setting for a wedding reception, and Nathanial Hardy, in spite of his reputation for miserliness, had spared no expense to make sure his only daughter's wedding reception would be the finest anyone in Avonlea could remember.

The hotel porches were draped and festooned with wreaths of wildflowers and pink roses, tied at intervals with fluttering silk ribbons. Long tables, covered with crisp white linen cloths and lavishly set with crystal and fine china, were set up on the lawns. White wicker chairs were placed strategically under spreading trees to offer a tiny oasis of comfort and shade.

Among all this finery sat the shiny yellow motorcar, almost on display, parked at the top of a hill that rolled towards the sea, complete with a sign draped on the back of it that read "Just Married."

Inside, in the great ballroom, the lavish reception was in full swing. An orchestra, brought all the way from Halifax, played heartily, and the marble dance floor was filled with swirling skirts and elegant dinner jackets. Sara watched, bright-eyed, from the sidelines, swept up in reminiscences of the many similar affairs her father had held in their own home in Montreal. Hetty stood fidgeting next to her, and Olivia was nervously surveying the crowd, trying to catch a glimpse of Mr. Hardy.

Clara Potts appeared from out of the crowd and took Hetty's gloved hand in her own. "I'm so glad you finally came to your senses, Hetty, and decided to come," she cooed.

Hetty snatched her hand away.

"For pity's sake, Hetty," said a rebuffed Mrs. Potts. "Don't be so standoffish." She peered around the room and then up at Hetty from under the bobbing roses on her hat, a sly smile on her face. "He's not going to bite you. As a matter of fact, on the contrary. He seems to be steering clear of you. I haven't seen hide nor hair of the man."

"That's fine with me," Hetty said tersely.

"Such a shame Rachel had to miss this. She's down with a touch of croup," remarked Mrs. Potts. "Must have been the cold night air." She looked at Hetty accusingly.

Hetty sniffed. It was no fault of *hers* if Rachel Lynde and Clara Potts wanted to wander around the village at all hours of the night. "So, there is divine justice after all," she couldn't resist adding.

Sara's sharp eyes spotted Mr. and Mrs. Hardy on the other side of the room, deep in conversation with a group of guests.

"There he is, Aunt Olivia. There's Mr. Hardy!" she whispered, prodding her aunt towards the proud parents of the bride. "Go and talk with him!"

Sara took Olivia's hand and literally pulled her through the dancing couples until they both stood at Mr. Hardy's elbow. He turned and smiled when he saw Olivia.

"Miss King!" he boomed. "How nice that you could come!"

Olivia smiled nervously, wondering if he would still feel that way after hearing what she had to say to him. "The reception is lovely Mr. Hardy, Mrs. Hardy."

Mr. Hardy put his great head closer to Olivia's ear. "It should be! The Hardy Steamship Company will have to double their business to pay for it." He leaned back and laughed uproariously.

Mrs. Hardy patted his arm as if to say "Enough is enough, dear," and fastened her attention on Olivia.

"I'm sure we'll get good coverage in our local paper with you in attendance, won't we, Olivia?" she asked sweetly.

Sara gripped her hand more tightly, and Olivia realized that she couldn't miss such an opening.

"Well, now, you know," she began nervously, hardly daring to look at Mr. Hardy's eyes, "I hate to mix business with pleasure...but I doubt there'll be an Avonlea *Chronicle* to carry the story of your daughter's lovely wedding, Mrs. Hardy."

"But that's dreadful!" exclaimed the proud mother. "You mean it's going out of business?"

"I'm afraid it looks that way," replied Olivia, gaining confidence. "You see, many of our local businesses have decided to advertise in a rival newspaper. And without advertising, the *Chronicle* is dead," she explained, quoting Mr. Tyler.

"But, how could that happen?" insisted Mrs. Hardy, bitterly disappointed at the prospect of no notice at all of the wonderful *fête* she and her husband had managed to pull off. "Why ever would local businesses stop advertising in it? It's just plain...traitorous!" she exclaimed, while her husband grew increasingly uncomfortable beside her.

Olivia turned to Mr. Hardy and smiled benignly. "Perhaps you could explain it to your wife, Mr. Hardy. I'm sure you had an extremely good reason, but it is the withdrawal of your company's advertising that's causing our paper to close."

Mrs. Hardy's eyes widened as she caught Olivia's meaning. "Nathanial?"

Mr. Hardy looked extremely embarrassed.

"May I speak to you...privately?" his wife said in a dangerously quiet voice.

Poor Mr. Hardy frowned and sighed, the

wind taken out of his sails, as his wife hustled him away.

Sara beamed up at her Aunt Olivia and shook her hand. Olivia bit her lip and giggled like a schoolgirl who's just pulled off the most outrageous prank without being caught. She was extremely proud of herself and felt sure the seeds of change had been sown.

Sara tugged at her sleeve once again and motioned with her eyes across the room. Olivia followed her gaze to see a tall, elegant man coolly survey the room and then proceed across the dance floor directly towards where her Aunt Hetty stood with Mrs. Potts.

"Look!" Sara whispered. "It's Romney Penhallow."

Hetty and Mrs. Potts were standing in the shelter of a potted palm, sipping fruit punch, when Mrs. Potts suddenly stiffened and jabbed Hetty in the ribs with her pudgy elbow. There, as large as life, coming towards them across the dance floor, was Romney Penhallow looking splendidly aloof in a white linen suit.

"He's coming towards us, Hetty," hissed Mrs. Potts. "I think he's going to ask you to dance!"

Hetty promptly turned her back on the approaching man. "I'd sooner dance with the devil," she snapped.

But, in spite of herself, Hetty looked over her shoulder as Romney approached. He smiled and looked directly into Hetty's eyes.

"May I have the pleasure of this dance..." He paused, and Hetty held her chin up stiffly and began to move forward. "...Mrs. Potts?" he finished.

Hetty's eyes darkened with surprise. Clara Potts's jaw dropped a mile as Romney politely took the punch glass from her hand.

"Excuse us," Romney said smoothly to Hetty.

Mrs. Potts recovered herself quickly and looked back at Hetty with raised eyebrows and the smallest hint of a self-satisfied smile on her face as she allowed herself to be whisked off onto the dance floor.

Left alone, Hetty found herself fighting with some very unexpected emotions. She was hurt, and more than a little jealous.

Elsewhere in the room, certain other emotions were also running high as Mrs. Hardy told her husband in no uncertain terms what she thought of his business dealings with the Avonlea *Chronicle*. She had had her heart set on a lovely wedding picture of her daughter on the inside page. Maybe even the front page! But now, thanks to him, this was not to be.

"But that's dreadful! How could you not support our local paper?" she demanded.

"Now, now, my dear," her husband said soothingly, hoping to calm her down.

"I'll tell you something, Nathanial," she said, her voice lowered to avoid any further embarrassment. "If you want to continue to have a happy home, you will switch your allegiance back to the *Chronicle* and have your business associates do the same!"

She turned abruptly and walked away, leaving Mr. Hardy to contemplate the grave implications of what she had just said.

Hetty was also about to leave the room when she felt a light tap on her shoulder. She spun around nervously and found her arm locked with Romney's as he led her firmly away from the dessert table. She gasped in protest, but he was not to be stopped.

"So, do you think we could attempt to have a

civilized conversation?" he asked lightly.

"If you're capable of having one," retorted Hetty, trying desperately to gather her wits.

"I am so pleased that you are not deaf," he commented, nodding pleasantly to a guest who had arched an eyebrow at the sight of them passing.

Hetty tossed her head. "When it comes to anything you might want to say to me, I *am* deaf."

He had led her to yet another punch bowl and, without letting go of his grip on her arm, he deftly filled a glass and offered it to her. Nearby, Mrs. Potts stood with a group of guests, obviously enjoying the verbal sparring.

"That's what I've always loved about you, Hetty, your open mind," he murmured, his voice heavy with sarcasm.

Hetty drew herself up and sipped daintily at the punch. "It is only equaled by the size of *your* self-regard," she retorted. "A man who is as wrapped up in himself as you are makes a very small package."

Romney chuckled. "Well, I see you haven't lost your talent for putting me in my place, have you, Hetty King?"

"And you haven't lost your knack for disgracing me in public," she countered icily.

Just as Hetty raised the glass of punch to her lips, Romney took it away from her.

"Oh, how I've missed our little talks," he said warmly.

Then, to Hetty's surprise, Romney put his arm around her waist and swept her onto the dance floor as the orchestra struck up a waltz.

Olivia and Sara watched, their eyes wide.

"I've never seen Aunt Hetty dance like that," said Sara.

"Oh my," said a breathless Olivia. "They seem made for each other!"

Romney and Hetty indeed danced as if they had been practicing for years, and the music and the battle of wits only served to bring out the sparkle in Hetty's eyes and the color in her cheeks.

"I find it absolutely unbelievable that you have remained in Avonlea all these years," Romney commented. "Haven't you ever wondered what you might be missing?"

"No," replied Hetty flatly, smiling smugly up at him.

Romney sighed and shook his head. "So like

an Islander. What a pity. Small-minded, pig-headed and unimaginative—and what's worse, proud of it!"

"How flattering of you to say so," replied Hetty, outwardly unperturbed, inwardly seething.

Olivia was so caught up in watching Romney and her sister that she barely noticed Mr. Hardy when he crossed the room and tried to get her attention.

"Miss King, do you have a moment?" he asked, his eyes cast downward.

As they whirled around the room, Romney eyed Hetty's upswept hairdo and, in particular, a tortoiseshell comb that seemed to be holding the entire weight of her elaborate coiffure.

"How is it that you have never married?" he asked, without taking his gaze from the orna-ment.

"I never found a man who was worth it," snapped Hetty. She was quite relaxed with this conversation by now and felt herself totally in control. In fact, she had forgotten how much she enjoyed dancing.

Her repose was short-lived. Romney took

hold of the comb and pulled it out with a flourish. A fall of Hetty's dark hair cascaded down
her back. She reached about wildly, trying to
restore it to its former position, but only suc-
ceeding in knocking her hat eskew.

"Romney!" she protested, but he went on
talking as if nothing had happened.

"Really? And I always assumed that, all these
years, it was because you'd never gotten over
me," he quipped.

Hetty pulled away from him, and as she did,
more of her hair came free and fell about her
face. She grabbed at it, trying to keep it on the
top of her head, as people around the couple
started to titter.

Hetty's face turned a furious shade of red
and anger started to flood through her. "How
dare you be so presumptuous?" she spat at him.
She turned on her heel and started out of the
room, twisting her long hair and trying to
restore her elaborate hairdo.

"I knew that once they started speaking,
things would be fine," Mrs. Potts was just in the
process of telling Sara when Hetty flew by them,
her hat jammed on her head, her hair in a state
of confusion.

Romney followed in pursuit. "Hetty! Come back!" he called, and Sara and Mrs. Potts just looked at each other and shrugged.

"I didn't realize I had started the ball rolling, but you must understand, the Carmody paper's prices are rock bottom. How could I refuse?" Mr. Hardy was earnestly explaining to Olivia as Hetty and Romney passed by them in a flash.

Olivia gasped, hardly able to keep her mind on what Mr. Hardy was saying to her. "Oh, I-I certainly see your point..." she stammered, wondering what in heaven's name her sister was up to.

Hetty went flying out onto the veranda, still trying to arrange her hair and keep her hat on her head, hoping against hope that no one had noticed her disarray.

"Hetty! Hetty King!" she could hear Romney shouting behind her. "Hetty, I want you to know that I forgive you."

Hetty whirled around in an absolute fury. "You forgive me?" she shouted, and then she immediately lowered her voice to a harsh whisper. "You should be on your knees begging *my* forgiveness!"

Romney looked truly puzzled. "Why in God's name would I be asking your forgiveness?"

"For humiliating me!" said Hetty. "All those years ago! Throwing me over for Rachel Lynde! Of all people!"

"Now, if Mr. Tyler were to lower his rate just slightly to show good faith, I'm sure we could talk..." Mr. Hardy paused, obviously waiting for some sort of response from Olivia.

But Olivia was gazing out the ballroom window to the porch beyond, completely distracted, hardly listening to a word Mr. Hardy was saying.

"Oh dear...not again..." she said helplessly.

Mr. Hardy thought she was remarking on the suitability of his plan. "You don't think he would be willing...?" he asked, thinking immediately of other strategies he could propose.

Olivia turned back to him, her face troubled.

"Oh...no...I didn't mean...Mr. Hardy, sometimes loyalties are more important than business! Will you excuse me?" she blurted out as she ran from the room in the direction of the porch.

Mr. Hardy watched her go and shook his head. "She drives a hard bargain," he remarked to himself.

Romney followed Hetty out onto the porch and attempted to take her arm once again to stop her. "Will you kindly stay in one place?" he asked.

Hetty shook off his arm. "Stop it! You're making a scene! Everyone's looking at us."

Another comb was hanging out of Hetty's hair and, to her horror, Romney plucked it out.

"If you would behave like a normal human being, they wouldn't be! Shall we dance?" He took her by the waist and twirled her around.

Hetty reached into her hat and pulled out a hat pin. She brought it down suddenly and stabbed him right in the bottom! He jumped and stifled a cry as Hetty looked at him triumphantly.

"I wouldn't dance with you again if my very life depended on it!"

She strode down the porch just as Olivia arrived, Mr. Hardy behind her. He touched Olivia's arm and she whirled around.

"Miss King," he said, "you're absolutely right!"

"About what?" asked a confused Olivia.

"Loyalties are more important than busi-ness!" He beamed at her.

Olivia followed her sister's progress down the porch, wondering what in creation the man was talking about!

Chapter Nine

Felix King had become totally bored with the reception and had grabbed a momentary lapse of attention on his mother's part to escape out-side. This was the chance he had been waiting for! He strode around the bright yellow car, looking at it with great admiration. Now that all the crowds were inside, he could marvel at it on his own, with no one pushing and shoving from behind and no one taller in front to block his view. He had never seen anything like it. He was absolutely mesmerized.

He looked towards the White Sands. No one around. Surely it wouldn't hurt if he just sat in it, just for a minute. He wouldn't touch anything, he promised himself. The temptation was too great, and within seconds of the thought cross-ing his mind, Felix opened the car door and slid in behind the wheel.

He looked closely at all the instruments and ran his fingers over the dashboard and the leather seats. He was in absolute heaven. But the sound of voices and running feet from the direction of the hotel brought him swiftly back to earth. He looked up to see his Aunt Hetty running along the porch. Felix's eyes widened with panic. Right behind her was the man who owned the motorcar!

Felix lost no time in jumping out, but he winced suddenly as he felt his knee scrape on something. Felix had unwittingly released the hand brake. The car rocked a little, but not enough to give him away as he took to the bushes and hid.

Hetty flounced down the steps of the White Sands Hotel and proceeded to walk towards the area where the car and the buggies were standing. She heard Romney behind her.

"Where are you going?" he was asking, in a voice that would melt butter.

Hetty decided that she couldn't leave just yet. She was bound and determined to let the scoundrel know exactly what she thought of him. She turned and faced him with all the dignity she could muster, despite the fact that her hat was askew and her hair resembled a bird's nest.

"You've embarrassed me enough for one day," she said quietly, glaring at him. "I'm leaving!"

"Well then let me drive you home," he said.

It was unbelievable, Hetty thought to herself. How could this man possibly make her such an offer after all he had said and done to her?

"Just you remember who you are underneath that fancy white suit, Romney Penhallow," she fumed. "Coming back to the Island to strut and show off, driving around in this revolting machine as if you owned the place!"

Romney took her arm and smiled at her annoyingly. "Thank goodness the roads around this devilish place aren't as narrow as your mind, Hetty."

Hetty brushed his hand away and stomped off, with Romney following behind.

From the porch, Olivia could see that things were not going well for Hetty. She pushed her way towards her through the gathering crowds, with Mr. Hardy at her heels, trying to get her attention.

"I was saying, Miss King, that loyalties are more important than business. You'll have my advertising back first thing Monday morning!"

Olivia stopped in her tracks, elated. "Oh that's wonderful Mr. Hardy. I can't thank you enough!"

But her heart was divided as she looked out onto the lawn, where a small crowd had gathered to watch the antics of Romney and Hetty. She knew there was going to be trouble, and she turned apologetically to Mr. Hardy.

"Thank you...thank you again!" she said breathlessly. "But if you'll excuse me!"

Olivia rushed across the porch. Mrs. Potts and Sara came out the doors and passed a perplexed Mr. Hardy, who had finally noticed the kafuffle on the lawn.

Hetty strode towards Romney's precious yellow motorcar and gave it a piercing stare that would have melted lead. "I wish you and this bucket of bolts would go right back to where you came from!" she yelled at Romney.

She glared at the car and gave the rear tire a good swift kick. The crowd gasped in disbelief as the car was set in motion. It started to roll slowly down the incline of the hill.

Romney stood transfixed, watching his car

gather speed as it rolled. Hetty's face went white. She couldn't believe what she had done.

People scrambled to safety as the car continued its fateful roll down the hill towards the sea. An unfortunate chef, carrying the wedding cake ceremoniously towards one of the beautifully set tables, looked around and, to his horror, saw the approaching car. He jumped aside, and in his haste he lost his balance and fell. The cake rose a foot into the air before coming down onto the grass with a splat beside him.

The table was next to go, and crystal and china flew everywhere. Olivia stared in disbelief. Hidden by the bushes, Felix covered his eyes and fled at the first available moment.

Poor Alice and Teddy Fraser were left in mid pose as the photographer spied the runaway car in his lens, grabbed his equipment and fled from its path. Alice immediately burst into the long-awaited tears.

"Edward! Don't just stand there. Go after it. You're younger than I am!" Romney shouted to the groom, so Teddy left his howling new bride and started off in pursuit down the hill. The car picked up even more speed as it drew ever closer to the ocean.

Teddy proved to be of not much use; he soon tripped and fell, and when he rose to his feet he stood wiping the dirt from his dinner jacket, leaving the motorcar to its fate.

Romney shook his head forlornly. "Good Lord. What's happened to the Penhallows?"

Then he proceeded to run after the car himself. Tables laden with pastries and punch bowls went helter skelter. Guests flew for safety in all directions as the car raced down the hill. Mrs. Hardy shrieked, and a dumfounded Mr. Hardy watched what his money had paid for go to ruin.

Their daughter ran to them and burst into yet more hysterical tears. "She's ruined my wedding!"

Romney ran down the hill as fast as his legs would carry him and finally came alongside his beloved vehicle. He leapt at it and ended up spread-eagled over the back of the car as he tried to jump in and throw the hand break on. Though it was difficult, he managed to get to the wheel and steer it away from the sea. He bounced over the brow of another small hill and promptly disappeared, car and all, into a haystack.

People at the top of the hill edged closer, Hetty included. There was a long, suspense-filled moment of silence, and then a white-trousered leg appeared, followed by an arm, and, at last, all of Romney Penhallow had materialized from the hay, his impeccable white suit tattered and filthy.

Hetty couldn't help herself. It was probably a nervous laughter, but the sight of him made her start to chuckle. People looked over their shoulders at her dubiously, unable to see the humor in the situation. The groom and Mr. Hardy glared. The bride was still in hysterics and not fit for anything, and her mother tried in vain to comfort her.

"There, there, Alice," she crooned. "You're making your face all red."

Olivia intercepted the look Mr. Hardy was giving her sister and hastened over to try to smooth things out a bit.

"I'm so sorry, Mrs. Hardy, Mr. Hardy. I'm sure my sister didn't mean to—" She didn't get any further.

"It could be a blessing in disguise that there is no Avonlea *Chronicle*," thundered Mr. Hardy, "for I promise you, if one word of this fiasco is printed, I'll make sure you don't have a job to go to, Olivia King."

"Mr. Hardy! Wait! I can explain," began Olivia, but Mr. Hardy gathered his family around him and walked quickly towards the White Sands.

Olivia sighed and turned to see Sara waiting for her, an extremely worried look on her face.

"I can't find Aunt Hetty anywhere," Sara said.

Chapter Ten

Olivia entered the now empty White Sands ballroom in a dither, flinging her wrap around her shoulders.

Sara was waiting for her. She could see that her aunt was furious, which was quite an uncommon thing for her to be.

"She is nowhere to be found!" Olivia said, her voice shaking with emotion. "And I'm not staying another minute. She'll just have to find her own way home." She sighed in frustration. "How could she do something like that? How could she ruin a wedding? I just can't fathom it!"

"It wasn't all her fault," said Sara.

Olivia looked down at her niece and took her

hand as they walked through the great ballroom doors and out of the hotel.

Romney Penhallow was still struggling with his car an hour after the incident. All the guests had either left or gone back inside the hotel. Some of the men had helped him push it from the haystack, and he had spent the remaining time cleaning it out. He was in the process of cranking the engine madly, with no results. He straightened his back and then crouched down to give it another energetic try. In mid crank, he suddenly lost all the strength in his arm. He gasped, as if struggling for breath, and collapsed backwards into the hay. He stared up into the sky with frustration, his face twisted.

Hetty poked her head out onto the porch of the White Sands, looking furtively around to make sure the coast was clear. All the guests appeared to have left. She breathed a sigh of relief, wrapped her shawl around her shoulders and walked quickly along the porch. She was startled to see that all the buggies had disappeared from where they had been parked.

"Deserted am I!" she exclaimed dramatically.

Fine thing! she thought to herself. At least Sara and Olivia could have waited.

But she straightened her back and set off down the road in her finery, trying not to think of the long walk home.

Hetty heard the unmistakable sound of Romney's car before she actually saw it. She kept walking, doing her best along the gravel road with her high-heeled kid shoes. Her hat was still askew and she had not even bothered to fix her hair. She set her jaw with determination as the sound grew inevitably closer and, finally, Romney drove right along beside her. Hetty kept on walking, her eyes straight ahead, her back erect.

"May I offer you a ride to Rose Cottage?" he asked politely.

Hetty responded with a stony silence.

"As you can see," he continued blithely, "it still runs."

"What a pity." Hetty couldn't keep herself from saying it.

Romney perceived this as progress. At least she was speaking to him!

"If it had been a horse, I probably would have had to shoot it," he said, attempting to make a joke, but his humor was rewarded with further silence. "Come now, Hetty, you can't walk all the way home."

"Hah!" she replied, not even looking at him as he rattled along beside her.

"Suit yourself, then!" he said, and, accelerating suddenly, he drove off.

Hetty hadn't expected him to leave so quickly. Once again she found herself alone in the middle of the road in the middle of nowhere. Rose Cottage was at least three more miles away. But she was certainly not going to let him get the best of her, and she trudged on.

A dog barked somewhere in the distance. A bee buzzed in her ear as it zipped by and, distracted by it, Hetty failed to look where her feet were going. Next thing she knew, she had tripped in a pothole and lost a shoe. The fine heel had broken off, too. She cursed to herself, put the shoe back on and threw the broken heel into the bush. Scowling, she hobbled around a corner and came face to face with Romney, who stood there, casually leaning against his car, obviously waiting for her.

"Give up?" he asked.

Hetty looked at him and, despite herself, felt a curious sense of relief. She shook her head and tried to control the small smile that was threatening to start at the corners of her mouth.

The yellow motorcar wound its way along a point of land that seemed to hang in space above the red cliffs and blue waters that ran as far as the eye could see. The "Just Married" sign still clung with a slight tilt to the back of the car.

Hetty found herself sitting back and actually relaxing, thoroughly enjoying the ride and the beautiful day. She had taken her shawl and put it around her head the way she had seen women in magazines do when traveling in motorcars. She realized now, as the wind from the sea blew in her face, it was not so much an affectation as a necessity.

Romney looked at her out of the corner of his eye. "My goodness, this brings back memories. You always were at your most content when you'd gotten even with me."

Hetty looked back at him, a look of challenge in her eye. "Anything you can do, I can do better, Romney Penhallow."

Romney smiled. "Is that so?"

Sara watched anxiously out the front window of Rose Cottage. She and Olivia had come home hours ago, and Hetty was still not back. Her Aunt Olivia had long since got over her initial anger and was just about to walk over to the King Farm to see if Hetty had by any chance gone there. Suddenly, Sara heard the sound of a car motor, and her mouth dropped open at the sight that met her eyes.

"Aunt Olivia!" she called. "Come quickly!"

What they saw was a motorcar moving at a steady pace along the road to Rose Cottage and pulling up in a cloud of dust.

"The brake! The brake!" Romney called out, a trace of nerves in his voice. "Down there! That's it!"

The car came to a shuddering stop, almost taking out the fence. Hetty King was in the driver's seat.

"That wasn't entirely bad...for a beginner," said Romney. "You could use a little practice with the brakes."

The two of them sat in the car in silence looking up at the sky, for want of something to do. Hetty felt uncomfortable. Her moment of bravado had passed and once again she was shy and stiff with the man sitting next to her. All of a sudden she felt him taking her hand in his. She snatched it away.

"I thought I'd drive along the coast tomorrow and do some sketching," he said casually. "Would you care to come?"

"Goodbye, Romney," said Hetty firmly, and she got out of the car before he had a chance to say anything more. He held her arm but she pulled away and walked towards the gate.

Romney swung out of the car and, catching her arm again, he swung her around to face him.

"Hetty, stop being so stubborn. Life is too short. We've already wasted more than thirty years. Do you want to waste thirty more? We don't have that kind of time. Hetty, for once in your life, let fate chart your course!"

Hetty just stared at him. "What rubbish!" she said, and, breaking away from him, she strutted up the walk. As she reached the porch steps, she turned and faced him. "My life was running its course in a most satisfactory manner, thank you, until you came along, and it will continue to do so after you leave!"

She turned and marched up the steps, but before she entered the house, Romney noticed that she couldn't help but glance back at him. Then she shut the door in his face. He smiled, not about to give up.

Sara and Olivia were all agog as Hetty entered the front hall of Rose Cottage.

"Hetty King, I am absolutely flabbergasted," Olivia burst out. "Never in my wildest imaginations could I ever have seen *you* driving a car!"

Hetty threw off her shawl and dropped it carelessly on the hall table.

"That's the trouble with you, Olivia, and everyone else in this town! They're narrow-minded and unimaginative. And what's worse, proud of it!"

Having said this and left her audience dumfounded, Hetty sauntered up the stairs.

Chapter Eleven

"You did what?" exclaimed Mr. Tyler.

Olivia stood facing her furious editor. "If what happened hadn't happened, it would all have turned out perfectly well...but—"

Mr. Tyler didn't give her time to finish. He stood up from his desk, almost knocking his chair over in the process. "This is my newspaper! Who gave you the right to go out and talk to Nathanial Hardy behind my back?"

"I was only trying to help! Someone had to do something!" stammered poor Olivia.

"For your information, I *was* doing something!" He picked up a sheet of paper from the top of a file cabinet and shoved it at Olivia. "I did a little sleuthing of my own. See this? This is what the Carmody publisher plans to charge next month."

Olivia scanned the piece of paper and looked up at Mr. Tyler with a furrowed brow. "But these rates are even with ours," she said.

"Exactly." Mr Tyler sat down again. "He couldn't afford to lower his rates any more than I could!"

Olivia couldn't for the life of her see what he was so upset about. This was good news. "So, now you'll be able to coax your advertisers back again!" she said cheerily.

To her surprise, Mr. Tyler rose angrily from his desk. "I would have been able to, if you and your confounded sister hadn't alienated all of them! Thank you very much, Olivia King! You've both been a great help!"

Olivia bit her lip, her dark eyes clouding. She could see his point.

Hetty and Sara walked smartly along the main street of Avonlea towards the general store.

Well, at least Hetty walked; Sara had to run to keep up with her. They were about to enter the store when Olivia pulled up on her bicycle.

"Hello, Sara," she mumbled as she set the bicycle against a railing and headed up the porch steps, without saying as much as one word to her sister.

Hetty exchanged an anxious glance with Sara, and they followed Olivia into the store.

"I'll be right with you, Olivia," called Mrs. Lawson from the back. Olivia stood at the counter, drumming her fingers. Hetty came and stood beside her.

"And to what do I owe this silent treatment, Olivia?" she asked coolly.

Mrs. Lawson bustled towards the counter and stopped discreetly, not wanting to appear to be eavesdropping, but listening just the same.

Olivia turned to her older sister, her cheeks flushed with annoyance. "Well, the Avonlea *Chronicle* is going to close, so you'll be happy to know that I failed in my attempts to save it."

"Your failure would hardly have given me pleasure, Olivia," sniffed Hetty, somewhat put out. "However, I did warn you that—"

"Oh Hetty! It was partly your fault and you

know it! Mr. Hardy won't even speak to me after all the trouble you caused at the wedding!"

"Oh...don't be ridiculous, Olivia," murmured Hetty, looking around and finding, to her further embarrassment, that Mrs. Lawson was working very hard at pretending not to listen to their conversation.

The storekeeper smiled ingratiatingly. "Is there something I can do for you ladies?"

"Yes, Elvira," said Hetty. She was about to add that she could mind her own business when she noticed Olivia looking around quite distractedly, the color in her cheeks rising higher and higher.

"I've forgotten what I came in for, Mrs. Lawson," said Olivia, and Hetty was sure that the next moment she would be stamping her feet in the same manner she had so often as a child. She almost smiled, but her expression froze as Olivia gave her a sharp glance. Sara made herself busy looking at the pattern books and hoped that the storm would soon blow over.

A buggy pulled up outside the store, and Felix and Alec King jumped down from it. Felix reached up to pat their horse, but it started and shied away as a great rattling sound came down the street. It was Romney in his yellow motorcar. He waved at them and tooted his horn.

"Whoa!" Alec said gently, calming his horse.

Felix looked at Romney's car with obvious relief. "Oh good! It still runs..." he mumbled to himself, and his father looked at him with some curiosity. "I mean...that's some motorcar, isn't it, Father?"

"It's a beauty, all right," said Alec, as he tied the horse to the railing.

"Do you think we'll ever have one like it?" asked Felix wistfully, watching as Romney pulled up in front of the store.

"Maybe someday, Felix," said Alec, walking slowly over to where Romney stood removing his goggles.

Alec put out his hand. "Romney Penhallow? That's quite a machine you got here! I'm Alec King, Hetty's brother. I'm sorry we didn't get a chance to meet at the party the other day...what with the, uh...all the commotion." Alec smiled as Romney pumped his hand up and down.

"Alec King! Of course." Romney grinned at Felix and pulled the boy's cap down over his eyes. "I remember you as a troublesome younger brother." He winked at Felix, who grinned back.

"I guess you could say I still am," said Alec, chuckling as he drew closer to the car. "I've been meaning to have a look at the future. You don't mind do you?"

Olivia came out of the store at that moment, Hetty and Sara following her. At the sight of Romney, they all stopped in their tracks.

Romney spotted Hetty out of the corner of his eye. "Did you know that your sister Hetty is a very commendable driver of this vehicle?" he said to Alec in a deliberately loud voice.

Alec looked up in surprise. "Hetty? Drive a motorcar?"

"That'll be the day," commented Felix wryly, unaware that his aunt was listening on the steps of the store, directly behind him.

Romney turned, making a pretense of noticing Hetty for the first time.

"Hetty!" he called. "There you are! I was just telling your brother what a fine driver you are."

Felix wheeled around. This car was going to get him into real trouble yet!

Hetty refused to take the bait and started to walk away up the street.

"Come on, Aunt Hetty!" shouted Felix after her. "Show us!"

Sara joined in the chorus. "Aunt Hetty? Please?"

Hetty showed no inclination to do anything of the sort. She continued on her way up the street.

"Betcha can't do it!" called Felix.

He had just spoken the magic words. Hetty stopped and turned and faced her nephew, looking him square in the eye.

"Can so, Felix King!" she said.

Hetty gathered her skirts and strode back towards the motorcar. Sara skipped along beside her. Hetty shoved her wicker basket into Felix's hands and, removing a scarf from around her neck, she proceeded to tie it about her hair as she walked with confidence to the bright yellow vehicle. Romney opened the driver's door with a flourish and, accepting his hand, Hetty climbed in behind the wheel.

Alec smiled and shook his head as he watched the proceedings. Romney rolled his sleeves up and gave the crank a robust turn. The engine jumped to life. By this time a little crowd of people had formed. The children ran to and fro with excitement, hooting and hollering. The women whispered behind gloved hands, and the men rocked back and forth on their heels.

Romney stepped gracefully up into the passenger seat, and Hetty put the machine into motion.

"Well, what do you know!" Alec exclaimed as the car made its way down the street.

The children ran along behind the car, shouting and clapping, delighted to see their teacher behaving in such an adventurous manner. Hetty couldn't help but smile. She was enjoying everything thoroughly, especially the shocked faces of the villagers who stared as she passed.

Rachel Lynde was walking along towards the general store when Hetty waved gaily to her. Rachel was dumbstruck! Could that possibly have been Hetty King, sitting up, large as life, next to Romney Penhallow? Driving a motorcar? And after she'd been told word for word by Mrs. Potts what had happened at the Hardy wedding? It was too much! She scurried towards the store. Obviously, she had some catching up to do. It didn't pay to get the croup in Avonlea. Life passed you by in the meantime!

Hetty drove along happily, every once in a while turning her head to look at Romney sitting next to her. She spotted Mr. Hardy himself marching along the main street towards them. She couldn't resist. She tooted the horn at him, and the poor man jumped a foot off the ground! After he had recovered himself, he shook his walking stick at the car.

"Look where you're going!" he called after her, and the crowd on the street tittered and waved.

Mrs. Lawson shook her head in disbelief as she stood next to Sara and Olivia on the porch of the general store. "And after the fuss she made about the motorcar in the first place...!" she said.

Rachel joined them, out of breath from running but blaming it on her recent illness. "That woman is as contrary as the weather!" she exclaimed. "But as I always say, all's well that ends well."

Chapter Twelve

The car was a bright yellow sunspot on the red gravel road as it wound its way around the bottom of a hill that dropped off into the sea. At the peak of the hill, on a patch of brilliant green lawn, was a lighthouse, painted white with a red diamond, facing out to the Atlantic. The road dipped away from it, and the car clattered across a little bridge over a mirror-like pond. Ferns and buttercups cascaded onto the road on either side, and here and there ripe strawberries were visible through the greenery.

Quite suddenly, Hetty came to a halting stop beside a field that rolled down to the grassy dunes of the beach. Before Romney could question why, she climbed out of the motorcar and started down the road, removing her scarf.

"Where do you think you're going?" Romney called after her.

Hetty turned to him, her face expressionless. "Your little joke is over," she said lightly. "I have no intention of staying."

Romney leapt nimbly over the car door, not bothering to open it. "Of course you're staying. I've brought a picnic lunch...for two."

Hetty watched, incredulous, as he withdrew a huge hamper from the back of the car. He threw an old patchwork quilt out onto the grass and began to straighten it and set things up.

"Of all the gall," Hetty exclaimed. "Really! How can you be so sure of yourself?"

Romney looked up from unpacking the hamper. "On the contrary, I'm not so sure of myself, especially where you're concerned." He thought for a moment. "Which is probably, I suppose, why I like you so much."

Hetty laughed nervously, not altogether displeased with his words. He motioned her over as if the entire question of her staying was dealt with and resolved.

"Roast chicken or lobster?" he asked. "I'm told the White Sands does a marvelous lobster."

Hetty sat. "Lobster, please."

Olivia had gone back into the general store after the excitement was over, Sara at her side. She had finally remembered what she had gone in for in the first place.

"And some of your camomile soap, and a pound of butter, Mrs. Lawson," she said.

"Aunt Olivia," Sara hissed, and she pulled on her aunt's sleeve. Olivia looked at Sara and then turned to where she was surreptitiously pointing.

Mr. Hardy was entering the store, still scowling from his run-in with the motorcar. He spotted Olivia and made a show of snubbing her, turning his back and walking to another area of the counter. Olivia could feel her temper beginning to rise. She gritted her teeth and followed him. She stood right next to him at the counter, making it absolutely impossible for the man to ignore her. Finally, he turned and glared at her.

Olivia smiled icily. "Good afternoon, Mr. Hardy."

"Good afternoon," he replied, his voice wooden.

"I don't suppose you'd be interested in some information I happen to have learned about the Carmody paper, would you?"

Mr. Hardy moved away from her rudely. "Not in the least."

Something in Olivia snapped, and her temper got the better of her. "Oh, I am so sick and tired of dealing with arrogant, belligerent, stubborn people!" she burst out angrily.

Mr. Hardy was aghast at the tone of her voice and stared at her, his own color beginning to rise.

Sara had never in her life seen her aunt so angry, except perhaps for that time she'd lit into Mrs. Potts and Mrs. Rae when they were spreading tales about how the fire had started in the town hall during Jasper Dale's magic lantern show.

Olivia tried to collect herself. "I'm sorry, Mr. Hardy..." she began, but he pasted an amused smile on his round, red face, and it only served to irritate Olivia further.

"Don't look at me that way, as if I'm a sweet little thing to be humored! I'm talking business here, whether you want to or not! Because, do you know what, Mr. Hardy? I have nothing to lose!" Olivia's voice rose, and her eyes flashed. By now, Mrs. Lawson, Sara and Mr. Hardy were her captive audience. "Now, which newspaper would you advertise in if the rates were identical, Mr. Hardy? Tell me that!"

"Why, the Avonlea *Chronicle*, of course," Mr. Hardy blustered.

Olivia slapped a piece paper into his hand. On it were written the up-and-coming rates of the Carmody paper that Mr. Tyler had given her.

"Well then," she said, tossing her head. "You'd better get over there before all the space is sold, because the Carmody paper is in trouble, too! And they're going to raise their rates right back up again. What do you think of that?"

Olivia gestured wildly upwards with her

hand and accidentally knocked a hanging basket full of onions all over Mr. Hardy. She stopped in shocked silence.

Mr. Hardy paused and began methodically to pick onion skins off his jacket.

"I've got to hand it to you, Olivia King," he said, looking her straight in the eye with a hint of a smile. "You and your sister certainly know how to make your point."

Chapter Thirteen

A soft breeze blew across the meadow, bending the daisies and the devil's paintbrushes in a graceful arc. Hetty made a grab for a napkin as it threatened to escape on the wind. She and Romney were finishing off their picnic lunch with tiny fresh strawberry tarts and lemonade. They sat in contented silence.

"Well, I suppose this is what it must feel like to be an old married couple," Romney observed.

Hetty started a bit, surprised, but not entirely disliking the turn of the conversation. She looked sideways at Romney as his brown hair blew across his forehead. She was amazed at how young he still looked. At that very moment, smelling the sweet, fresh scent of the grass and the salt sea air on the breeze, she could swear that the thirty years had not gone by. So many picnics they had shared, together, and with their friends. So many years ago.

Romney got up and took a sketch pad and charcoal from the hamper. He settled down and gazed out at the deep blue of the sea. When he spoke, it was almost as if he had read her thoughts.

"There's nowhere quite like this island, Hetty. I'd forgotten how much I love this infernal place. I've never had so much pure enjoyment out of life as I have in the past few days."

"Mostly at my expense," Hetty couldn't help commenting, a smile on her face.

"Oh come now, Hetty, you got your own back," said Romney, leaning back on his arm, looking at her with his sardonic smile and starting to sketch. "You know, if I had stayed in Avonlea, I probably would have pursued you and married you. You're the only girl I knew who had her wits about her, and you still are. I have a great affection for you."

A huge lump caught in Hetty's throat. For a moment she was afraid that her feelings were going to betray her. "I have a fondness for you as well." She instantly felt she had said too much, and added, "When you're not trying to be something you're not." She certainly didn't want to give in entirely to this tack in the conversation.

"Our greatest pretenses are built not to hide the evil and the ugly in us, but our emptiness," he said grandly and then smiled with a tinge of sadness. "Some poet or another said that."

Hetty looked at him oddly, his sudden change of mood a puzzle to her. He looked up at the sky.

"The light is incredible on this island. Different from anywhere else on earth." He turned back to his sketch pad and began to draw.

"Why did you never come back here until now?" The words were uttered before she could stop herself. A question that she had buried so deeply, so many years ago. What is wrong with me? Hetty thought to herself in anguish.

Romney turned to Hetty and regarded her in a quizzical manner. "Guilt...I suppose."

"Guilt?" she repeated. She'd always had her own theories, but guilt was not part of them.

"I jumped ship...I abandoned my father

when he needed me most. My mother never let me forget it to her dying day."

"You didn't abandon him. You went to art school," said Hetty practically.

Romney smiled appreciatively at her support and then looked back out to sea. Hetty couldn't help thinking how she liked the way his eyes crinkled in the corners when he smiled like that. Laugh lines, she thought.

"Hetty, you remember how sick he was, even before I left. My mother felt it was a son's duty to stay by his father's deathbed, even at the expense of his own dreams. I couldn't do it."

"And a good thing, too," Hetty interjected. "What a waste of talent that would have been."

"Ah, yes," he said, sitting forward and looking her right in the eye. "But you would never have done such a thing, would you, Hetty? You probably looked after both of your parents, didn't you?"

Hetty looked away. "Yes. That was my duty. And...my choice."

"At great sacrifice," he stated emphatically, and then laid back on the grass. "I have never been very good at sacrifice. Strange, though, how life has a way of exacting punishment for our deeds. Well, whatever happens, I swear I will never hold anyone hostage to my death...my needs."

"What do you mean?" asked Hetty.

"I mean that I'd prefer to die privately, without burdening anyone."

Hetty was incredulous. "Not even...a loved one...to see you through?"

Romney sat up and removed his sketch from the sketch board. "Especially not...a loved one."

Hetty looked at him, still wondering what he meant and not entirely liking the new direction the conversation seemed to have taken. She supposed it was natural, however, that the Island would stir up all these old memories for Romney.

"I have to admit, Hetty K., I didn't come back to Avonlea solely to see you, but now I realize it was the best reason of all."

Once again a jolt of emotion passed through Hetty and threatened her composure. She felt embarrassed and elated at the same time, and she covered her confusion by cleaning up the picnic things. She tried to rise, but Romney took her arm.

"No, don't escape. I wanted to say that to

you, my friend. And for once, let me have the last word on the subject."

Romney took Hetty's chin and kissed her on the cheek. A sudden gust of wind caught some of his sketch paper from his board and it started blowing across the field. Hetty pulled away and, rising quickly to her feet, chased after it.

"Let it go," Romney called after her, but he rose as well and went to join her. "Do you remember how we used to run all summer long in our bare feet through these fields?"

Hetty laughed and walked back to him, waving some sheets of paper in her hand. "I'd never wear shoes if I could help it!"

Romney grinned and glanced down at her boots and heavy skirt. "I dare you to do it again."

Hetty looked at him defiantly and instantly sat down in the grass and took off her boots and stockings. He did the same.

"Race you, Romney!" she called as she took off across the field.

Romney threw his head back and laughed. Then he chased her through the grassy meadow. As she ran through the long grass, Hetty could feel the spirit of her youth break free from all the layers she had contrived to cover it with over the years. How good it felt!

They ran down to the grass-covered dunes, laughing and calling to each other. Hetty, as always, was the faster of the two, and the distance between them grew until she was quite a bit ahead of him. She turned around, laughing, out of breath, and discovered he was nowhere to be seen.

Romney had run along the uneven ground of the dunes, slipping and sliding on the sand. Hetty had disappeared among the long grass of the hills and gullies. Suddenly, Romney's face twisted with a jolt of pain and his legs gave way. He fell heavily to the ground, hidden by one of the dunes.

"Romney! Where are you?" he could hear Hetty's voice calling in the distance.

He desperately attempted to stand. He didn't want her to find him like this, under any circumstances.

Hetty walked along the beach, still calling, becoming more and more puzzled. "Romney! Where are you? I know you're hiding!" she called, the beach echoing with the games of hide-and-seek of long ago.

She rounded a dune and looked down in surprise. There was Romney, lying in the sand, grinning up at her sheepishly.

"I tripped in a blasted groundhog hole!" he said blithely.

Hetty snorted with laughter. "Don't give me that. You just couldn't keep up with me!"

Hetty held out her hand for him to grab and they walked, arm in arm, back to the field, Romney limping only slightly.

"So, to make a long story short," Olivia said as she cheerfully cleared the table of the dinner dishes, "Mr. Hardy put his advertising back in the Avonlea *Chronicle*!"

"I knew you could do it, Aunt Olivia," cried Sara, giving her aunt a well-deserved hug.

Olivia had proudly filled Hetty and Sara in on what had happened in the general store and at the subsequent meeting she had held with Mr. Hardy and Mr. Tyler.

"Well, I didn't exactly take over the paper, Sara, but Mr. Tyler did hint that he might be willing to take me on as a partner!"

"There, you see, Olivia? I told you, you were worrying over nothing," said Hetty, virtually dancing around the kitchen, putting away the plates and silverware one minute, adjusting the flowers in the middle of the table the next. "One has to take chances in this life," she crowed. "If you don't, well, they may not come along again. Now remember that, Sara."

Sara looked at her Aunt Olivia and winked. "Like learning to drive a motorcar?"

It was clear to Sara that something had happened to her Aunt Hetty that afternoon. She hadn't said a word, but both Sara and Olivia knew that there was something up. Hetty was acting like a girl, and the physical transformation was quite amazing. Her cheeks were pink, her eyes were bright—everything about her was just, more alive, Sara thought.

Hetty turned and stared at Sara. "Driving a motorcar, my auntie," she retorted. "Don't you think it's your bedtime?"

Then she turned to Olivia and laughed, putting her arms around both of them. Olivia and Sara exchanged knowing glances. Hetty King had dropped at least twenty years that day.

Chapter Fourteen

Dawn was just breaking, and the roads around Avonlea were deserted. In the early morning light, the mist rose from the fields like ghosts, and there was an ominous, yellowy gray pallor along the horizon that might warn a sailor of bad weather ahead. Black-and-white cows stood perfectly still in the dew-laden fields—a sure sign of rain.

The silence was broken by the unexpected sound of a buggy traveling along the road. Alec King was getting an early start to a sale in Markdale. He was thinking of buying a new plow and had heard there was one in almost-new condition up for bidding. Alec loved the feeling of being the only one on the road, and he looked around with great satisfaction. He never tired of this road and its views. It had just crossed his mind that it might rain before the day was out when he came over the brow of a hill and saw a buggy in the ditch at the bottom of it, one of its wheels off. He recognized Dr. Blair standing beside it, and Alec smiled as he watched the good man give the wheel a vicious kick. The doctor looked up with a mixture of relief and embarrassment as Alec came to a stop beside him.

"Dr. Blair, you're on the rounds early this morning. What's the trouble?"

"Oh, thank goodness you're out and about, Alec. My wheel has come off and I've got an emergency to get to." He was obviously agitated and kept looking at his pocket watch.

"Hop up," said Alec. "I'll give you a lift. Where are you headed?"

A grateful Dr. Blair scrambled into the buggy. "The White Sands Hotel. I'm much obliged, Alec."

Hetty looked at her reflection in the mirror over the table in the front hall of Rose Cottage. She picked up yet another new hat and adjusted it on her head, testing one angle and then another. The emerald green became her. It brought out her eyes, she thought. She heard a slight movement on the stairs and looked around, startled that anyone else would be up at this time of the morning. Sara sat on the stairs in her nightgown.

"You're up early, Sara," remarked Hetty, deciding on an angle and thrusting a hat pin through to hold it steady.

"I heard you up," said Sara. "Where are you going?"

"Oh, I'm having breakfast at the White Sands," replied Hetty, satisfied with the result.

"With Mr. Penhallow?" Sara asked.

"That's right. He's picking me up," said Hetty, and she turned to her niece, noticing for the first time the hint of anxiety on the child's face.

"Aunt Hetty..." Sara began, and then she hesitated.

"Yes? What is it?" asked Hetty, giving her niece her full attention.

"Do you think what they're saying in town is true?" Sara looked up at her aunt, her blue eyes full of serious thoughts.

"What are their tongues wagging about now?" asked Hetty, with a toss of her chin just to let Sara know that, whatever it was, it wouldn't bother her or worry her in the least.

"That you might marry Romney...and leave Avonlea."

Hearing the words "marry" and "Romney" in the same sentence shocked Hetty a bit. She didn't know whether to be ecstatic or terrified. Certainly it did her ego good to know that Avonlea gossip was centering on things that, up to this day, had never been considered possibilities for Hetty

King. She looked sharply at Sara and realized the child was truly worried.

"Sara...a truce should never be confused with an engagement..." she began, searching for the right words.

"It's more than a truce," said Sara quietly, twisting her nightgown around her little finger.

Her Aunt Hetty had been stepping out steadily with Romney Penhallow for almost two weeks now. Everyone was talking about it. And she seemed so happy. And of course if they did decide to get married, Romney would never want to stay on the Island. Not when he traveled all over the world. Mrs. Lynde had even joked about how much he hated Avonlea and couldn't wait to be out of it. They were all amazed he had stayed as long as he had.

Sara felt conflicting emotions raging inside her. She wanted her Aunt Hetty to be happy. She truly did. But, what would happen to her, Sara? Feelings of great insecurity had swept over her the past few days. She had just got used to her life in Avonlea. She was just beginning to get over the first crushing despair of her father's death, and she loved living with Hetty and Olivia. She knew that Olivia would not always be there; she was still young, and bound to find a husband, as her cousin Felicity had put it. But what if Hetty left too? Who would she live with then?

Hetty sat down on the stairs next to Sara. "Very well...it is more than a truce. You're right about that." She hugged Sara. "But I'm not about to leave Avonlea...or you. Lord knows, Olivia couldn't handle you on her own."

She tousled Sara's hair and gave her a light kiss on the head. "Now, go back up to bed, or feed the chickens, one or the other."

Sara smiled and hugged her aunt back. It was wonderful how, every once in a while, a grown-up could read your thoughts...and not just when your head was full of mischief!

Chapter Fifteen

A hotel porter came quickly down the stairs and crossed the reception area of the White Sands Hotel, his heels clicking on the freshly polished floor. In his hand was a sketch board. He passed in front of the great stone fireplace that dominated the hotel entrance and approached a man sitting in a wheelchair, his head bowed down to his chest. He lay the board across the man's lap and backed away, obviously not knowing quite what else to do. He nodded to Alec King, who sat across from the man, and took his leave.

From behind the reception desk came Dr. Blair. He motioned to Alec, who rose and joined him.

"This is a merciless neurological disorder," the doctor said in low tones. "Once you start to slip, you degenerate quickly. He shouldn't really even be moved when he has an attack."

He walked over to where the man sat. His hands shaking violently, the man didn't seem to be aware of the doctor's presence until he spoke to him directly.

"All the arrangements have been made, Mr. Penhallow. An ambulance coach will arrive momentarily, and someone will pick up your car and make sure it is safely transported to Montreal within the week." He paused and then went on. "But I do wish you'd reconsider traveling, for a few days at least."

Romney looked up at Dr. Blair with great difficulty. His face was lined with pain, and he seemed to have lost control of its muscles.

"I would have been much more comfortable in my own vehicle." He struggled with the words. "Besides, the way I drive, it would have been faster." He gave a chuckle. "And, as we all know, time is running out."

"Oh...well...I wouldn't say that, Mr. Penhallow," Dr. Blair said awkwardly.

Even in his rapidly declining condition, Romney managed his sardonic smile. "Don't use your bedside charm with me," he said gruffly. "I realize I'm on the way— how do they put it?—to the other side. I know well enough from my father's experience."

"I remember reading about your father's case. My predecessor had never treated a neurological disorder of that severity." Dr. Blair stopped, realizing that he most likely had said too much.

Romney's head dropped again, in fatigue. "Ah yes...my father's legacy to me," he mumbled.

"I'm sorry," was all the doctor could think of saying. "Well, I shall see if all is ready," he said, and he hastily made his exit.

Alec once again sat down opposite Romney.

The grandfather clock ticked the hours away loudly in the front hall of Rose Cottage. Hetty entered the hall and looked at the time. She sighed with frustration and went out the door to the front porch. Her veil was in place, covering her new hat, all ready to go. She had been ready to go for two hours. She peered down the road in both directions, willing the sound of a motor-car to reach her ears.

"Where is he?" she said under her breath, her mood ricocheting back and forth between anger and anxiety.

When Olivia came out to shake the table-cloth, she found her sister pacing up and down the porch nervously.

"Oh, good Lord!" exclaimed Hetty, not particularly wanting to be seen by anybody.

Olivia looked at her in surprise. "I thought you'd already left, Hetty," she said.

Unable to look at Olivia, Hetty clung to the porch railing and tried to hold back sobs that were threatening to overtake her.

"Romney should have called for me two hours ago. Oh Olivia, clearly I must be a fool. How could I be so stupid as to have fallen into the same trap all over again? He's probably deliberately led me on only to humiliate me...again!"

Olivia approached her sister and put her hand sympathetically on her arm. "Hetty, he wouldn't do that."

Hetty squared her shoulders and viciously wiped away the few tears that had managed to escape. "Oh yes he would!" she stated flatly, her voice full of the old need for revenge. "But he's not going to get away with it."

As Olivia watched, Hetty strode from the porch in the direction of the back shed.

"Peter Craig!" she called. "Bring that horse around and hitch it up to the buggy!"

Alec King sat quietly in the White Sands reception hall, knowing intuitively that what the man opposite him probably wanted most was silence. But Romney, aware that they were alone, raised his head and leveled his gaze at Alec.

"Alec King," he said in a labored voice, "I am pleased that fate placed you in Dr. Blair's service this morning. There is something I would like you to do for me."

"Of course." Alec leaned forward in his chair and Romney continued.

"Please explain to your dear sister, Hetty...

about my sudden, rude departure...I could never burden her with this..."

"I hope she'll understand," muttered Alec. "Knowing Hetty, she would have wanted to see you herself."

A trace of his usual humor returned to Romney's face. "No, I care...far too much for her..." he managed to say. "I want her to remember me the way I was, not as I have become. Besides," he added, "her sense of duty is far too strong. I'd never get out of here..." He forced a smile and looked up at Alec. "I know Hetty pretty well, too, you know."

Alec smiled back, and looked up to see Dr. Blair once again approaching them.

"Everything's ready, Mr. Penhallow," the doctor said, quietly. "I'll take you out now."

Dr. Blair pushed Romney's wheelchair gently towards the front door. Just as they reached it, Romney handed a package to Alec.

"For Hetty...please, Alec."

"Of course," said Alec, and he gave him a bit of a salute as the doctor wheeled him out the door.

Chapter Sixteen

Hetty drove to the White Sands at as fast a clip as she dared and reached its gates in record time. She found a spot to leave the buggy, disconcertingly close to the bright yellow motorcar. She glared at it, hesitated and then went to give it a kick, but she thought better of it and instead headed determinedly towards the front door of the hotel.

Once inside she went directly up to the clerk at the desk.

"Yes, madam. May I help you?" asked the young man politely.

"Yes. I would like you to inform Mr. Penhallow that Miss Hetty King would like to speak with him," said Hetty grandly.

The clerk suddenly looked quite distressed. "I'm afraid that's not possible, madam. Mr. Penhallow is no longer staying in the hotel."

"Oh yes he is, young man," said Hetty, greatly irritated. "His car is outside for all to see!"

"Yes, I realize that, madam," stammered the poor clerk. "But if you'll just let me explain..."

Hetty looked him straight in the eye with an icy stare. "I demand to speak to him!"

The clerk began to edge his way out from behind the desk, looking more and more out of his depth with the situation. "Perhaps madam would be good enough to wait here for just one moment, and I'll see if the manager is free to talk with you?"

"I do not wish to speak to the manager! I wish to speak with—" said Hetty in exasperation, losing her patience entirely, but the young man had disappeared into an inner office.

She rolled her eyes in frustration and began to pace in front of the desk. As she turned towards the entrance, she was greatly taken aback to see Alec and Dr. Blair coming towards her.

"Dr. Blair, what in heaven's name are you doing here? Alec?"

In spite of her protests, the two men led her over to a chair in the reception area and sat her down.

"Hetty, I am sorry," said Dr. Blair, patting her shoulder. "Alec, thank you for all your help. I'll leave you two."

Hetty sat stock-still in the chair, trying to take in and accept everything Alec and Dr. Blair had told her.

"Why did Romney leave, without saying goodbye?" she asked, in a voice that was barely audible.

Alec took a deep breath. "Hetty, he was in very bad shape. You remember how his father was."

Hetty was struck with a sudden realization. "His father! Oh Lord, his father, of course!"

Alec looked at his sister, his face lined with worry.

"He told me. Oh, how could I have been so blind? That's what he was trying to tell me! Alec, I should have helped him. I know I could have..."

"He knew that, Hetty. But you'd have met your equal trying to help Romney Penhallow," Alec said reassuringly. "He said he wanted you to remember him as he was. He cared for you deeply."

Hetty smiled at him, trying her best to keep the tears that were just below the surface from flowing. Alec handed her the package Romney had given to him.

"He asked me to give you this."

Hetty took it with shaking hands

"Come on. Let me take you home," Alec said gently.

"No..." Hetty replied. "I'd just like to sit for a minute...on my own."

Alec clasped her hand, rose and looked down at his sister with some concern. She looked up at him gratefully.

"Thank you, Alec," she said sincerely. "I'm glad you were here."

He squeezed her shoulder and walked away.

Hetty heard the doors close after him and, despite herself, she started to cry. She clutched the package, looked down at it and slowly began to untie the string around it. With trembling hands, Hetty drew away the paper and stared down at a familiar image. It was a sketched portrait of herself, beautifully classic in its design. The tears flowed relentlessly and the image blurred.

Chapter Seventeen

The rosy glow of summer had given way to autumn's ruddier hues, and the roses that wound their way in profusion around the trellises of Rose Cottage had taken on colors of a more subtle nature. Deep reds were now a smoky rose, bright yellows a more ambiguous peach. There was a depth of feeling in the air itself that had been missing in the bright days of summer.

A sudden coolness outside had prompted Hetty to light a fire in the hearth in the parlor. She rose after giving the logs a bit of a push to come eye to eye with her portrait, now framed and sitting on the mantle. She adjusted it ever so slightly.

Rachel Lynde sat comfortably ensconced on the sofa in front of the fire, cup of tea in front of her, reading the Avonlea *Chronicle*.

"It's my opinion that this newspaper has come a long way since Olivia applied her hand to it," she said matter-of-factly.

"Hmm," said Hetty distractedly, her gaze still resting on the drawing, noticing how the mottled glow of the flames threw interesting shadows upon it.

"Even the death notices are worded nicely!" continued Rachel, and she went back to reading. "Well, what do you know!" she announced. "Atossa Phipps has finally passed on." She looked up at Hetty over the top of her wire-rimmed spectacles. "She's been dying for years."

Rachel buried her nose once again, and Hetty

ran her finger over the top of a bookcase looking for dust that had escaped her cleaning.

Rachel looked up quickly at her friend, her mouth open, a look of sincere shock on her face. Then she peered back at the words in the news-paper that had jumped out at her seconds before. She fastened a look on Hetty once again, and then back to the paper, and then back to Hetty, studying her with her mouth still open.

"Well, as I live and breathe!" she said quietly.

Hetty glanced down at her, noticing her shocked face. "What is it Rachel?"

Rachel took a deep breath. She wasn't accus-tomed to being caught by surprise, and she didn't enjoy the feeling one bit.

"Hetty! I hardly know how to tell you this..." She paused, wondering how to go on. "Romney Penhallow has passed away! In Montreal!"

Hetty spoke quietly, with no emotion appar-ent in her voice. "I know."

Rachel was oblivious to Hetty's real feelings, so carefully were they hidden after weeks of practice.

"Well, isn't that just like him!" she expostu-lated. "Dying without so much as a goodbye. Just like he left the Island."

Hetty picked up a book from the shelf and made a great pretense of leafing through it. "That's not quite the case Rachel..." she said quietly.

"Well, what in heaven's name did he die of? It doesn't say here. It wouldn't surprise me if his outlandish lifestyle killed him! These artists you know..." she said insinuatingly. Rachel didn't know a thing about artists or their lifestyles, but it served her purpose at the moment to seem as if she did.

To anyone else, it would have been obvious that Hetty didn't really want to discuss the matter further. "No, it wasn't that..." was all she said, and she replaced the first book and picked up a second.

"I shouldn't speak ill of the dead," continued Rachel relentlessly, "but I still can't get over how he left you in the lurch...and now this!" She flicked the newspaper with her hand. "I certainly don't regret the day I interfered between you two. The man was a scoundrel," she said decisively, and then added for good measure, "God rest his soul."

From the darkened corner where she stood with the book pressed between her hands,

Hetty couldn't help but speak up in defense of Romney.

"He was a good man, Rachel...and I will miss him."

Rachel went on as if Hetty hadn't spoken. To give her the benefit of the doubt, her hearing was not what it used to be, and she had been so busy listening to herself that she could very well have missed what Hetty had said entirely.

"Well, there's one thing we can always count on with you, Hetty," she said vehemently. "You might lose your head in a crisis, but you always come right straight back to earth once you come to your senses. I'm glad you've got him out of your system."

Hetty had the brief and tantalizing desire to laugh, but she felt she must set the record straight, no matter what it cost.

"Rachel..." she began, and this time Rachel listened. "Romney and I have been exchanging letters, ever since the day he left."

Rachel's jaw dropped. "Exchanging letters! Well, aren't we full of surprises? That's not like you."

"Need I say, many things in this life aren't always as they appear?"

Hetty turned away, and as Rachel would say afterwards, whenever she recounted this story, "It was as if a cloak of mystery fell round about Hetty King's sensible shoulders."

Rachel stared at her friend. "Don't talk in riddles, Hetty. All I know is that you and the entire King family have been mighty close-mouthed about this whole situation. You can't be totally unaware of what the town has been saying over the past month."

"I don't think I particularly care," replied Hetty simply.

Rachel was not going to stop at that. "They're saying he threw you over, that's what! Not that I, as your friend, entered into such idle chit-chat, of course."

Hetty looked at her and smiled wryly. "No. Of course not."

Rachel looked up, unsure once again whether Hetty's tone of voice was totally sincere. Hetty was aware what agony Rachel was going through. For Rachel, not knowing the whole story was to suffer a fate far worse than death.

"Well, Rachel." Hetty sighed and continued. "If it will satisfy you, Romney came back to this island to see it one last time...to say goodbye."

She broke off, as the emotion she was trying so hard to keep in check threatened to break through. She picked up her cup of tea to hide her feelings.

Rachel was being so careful not to interrupt Hetty that you could have heard a pin drop.

"And he did not throw me over," said Hetty. "Quite the opposite, in fact."

Rachel looked as if she could have been knocked over with a feather, and she waited expectantly for more details. When none were forthcoming, she prodded.

"Really? But think of all the talk there's been! Why didn't you say something...anything?"

Hetty smiled and poured herself more tea. She sat down next to her friend on the sofa. "Because I knew that you, Rachel, in your own inimitable way, would know best how to spread the truth. That is what friends are for, isn't it?"

Rachel slowly took off her spectacles as the full reality of the situation, as she perceived it, dawned on her.

"Hetty," she said, bowing her head in remorse, "when I think what I put you through, I'm amazed you're still my friend. I'm sure you'll never forgive me."

"What? For reintroducing the two of us?" Hetty shook her head. "Oh no, Rachel. On the contrary. I can't thank you enough."

Hetty patted a perplexed Rachel on the shoulder and stared into the fire, thinking of laughter and picnics and running barefoot through fields like a child again, waist-high in the grass. And, of course, the sheer bliss of driving a bright yellow motorcar beside a man whose eyes crinkled at the corners when he laughed. Oh yes, she thought, for once, she, Hetty King, had let fate take its course, and she thanked her lucky stars that she had.

Hetty and Rachel sat side by side in front of the fireplace, thinking their own thoughts as they watched the dance of the flames and listened to the comforting crackle of the fire.

❦   ❦   ❦

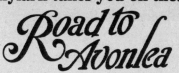